Sleuthing on the Set

I let the script drop onto my lap, put my head back against the couch, and closed my eyes. I tried to imagine how it would feel to be Esther Rackham. What reaction must she have had to finding a badly wounded man out in the middle of nowhere?

Esther's brothers were infamous criminals, two young men known as the Rackham Gang. I was never sure why they were called a gang, since there was just two of them. And criminals or not, Esther must have loved them. Did she know they were going to pull off the heist at the Mahoney Anvil Company? Was she planning to meet them somewhere out near the cave? Or maybe she'd gone there to try to stop them. . . .

I let out a sigh. It was no use. I was supposed to be trying to think of Esther's feelings, and instead I was thinking of the mystery!

NANCY DREW
girl detective

Available from Aladdin Paperbacks

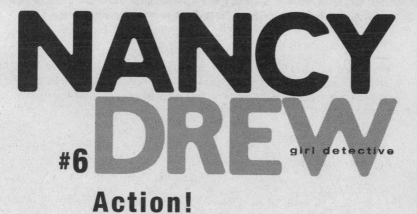

NANCY DREW

girl detective

#6

Action!

CAROLYN KEENE

Aladdin Paperbacks
New York   London   Toronto   Sydney

First Aladdin Paperbacks edition July 2004

Copyright © 2004 by Simon & Schuster, Inc.

ALADDIN PAPERBACKS
An imprint of Simon & Schuster Children's Publishing Division
1230 Avenue of the Americas, New York, NY 10020

Manufactured in the United States of America
20 19

NANCY DREW and colophon are registered trademarks of
Simon & Schuster, Inc.

NANCY DREW: GIRL DETECTIVE is a trademark of
Simon & Schuster, Inc.

Library of Congress Control Number 2004103214

ISBN-13: 978-0-689-86571-8   ISBN-10: 0-689-86571-6

0611 OFF

Contents

The Reluctant Star

Nancy Drew leaving waffles on her plate?" Hannah Gruen cried. "I don't believe it!"

I jumped, startled. Hannah was leaning over to take away my breakfast plate, filled with a half-eaten waffle and two strips of bacon. I snatched up my fork to finish eating. "Sorry," I mumbled. "I must've been daydreaming."

Hannah smiled and headed off to the kitchen to get my father his usual second cup of coffee. I took a bite of the homemade waffles. Hannah is officially our housekeeper, but she's also a terrific cook, and one of my favorite people in the world. But somehow Hannah's delicious waffles weren't holding my interest this morning. I was worried. More than worried. I was downright terrified.

My fork dropped to the plate as I pictured the day ahead—a day that was sure to make me the laughingstock of the city of River Heights!

". . . Nancy. Dad paging Nancy," my father was saying. I glanced up at him in surprise. How long had he been talking to me?

"Sorry," I said again.

Dad studied me with narrowed eyes. I recognized the expression; it was the famous Carson Drew sizing-up look. My father is one of the most prominent lawyers in town, and part of being a good lawyer is knowing how to read people. He can tell what anyone is thinking just by watching them for a few minutes. I'm good at that too. It comes in handy when I'm solving a mystery, and that means it comes in handy a lot.

But this morning the only case on my mind was the mystery of how to turn myself into an actress.

"Thinking about your scenes for today?" Dad guessed.

I nodded. "I've been working on memorizing my lines," I said. "But I still don't feel ready." I had recently taken a part in *Stealing Thunder,* a movie being filmed in town. It was a recounting of one of the most famous events in the history of River Heights: the great River Heist, in which a gang led by the Rackham boys stole a fortune from the local manufacturing baron, an anvil maker named Ethan Mahoney. It has remained a mystery, because no one ever found out what became of the Rackham boys—or the money—after the heist. I was playing Esther Rackham, the sister of the two Rackham boys, and that suited me just fine. Esther was my kind of girl. She'd tried her best to keep her brothers from committing the robbery.

Dad patted my hand. "It's normal to have a few stage fright jitters," he told me. "But you'll do fine."

"It's just . . ." I wasn't sure how to describe my feelings. Usually I'm very self-confident. But faced with the idea of acting in front of a camera, I felt nauseated. I had done a few scenes the week before when the production first got under way, and I'd found it difficult to act natural while the cameras were rolling. "I'm not an actor," I finally said.

Dad grinned. "Sure you are," he told me. "Every time you go undercover on a case or sweet-talk information out of someone, you're acting."

"Sort of," I said. "But it's not the same. I'm solving a mystery. It's always about getting answers and finding out the truth. In this movie the whole point is *not* to tell the truth. I have to pretend to be someone I'm not."

"Sounds like fun," Hannah commented, coming back in with Dad's coffee.

"Maybe that's the problem," I replied, trying to lighten up. "I'm not used to doing anything just for fun."

"Well, you've already solved one mystery on this film," Dad said. "I think you're due for some relaxation and fun."

He was talking about a mystery I'd unraveled just a few days before. *Stealing Thunder* had been on the verge of collapse because the continuity chief and one of the lead actors were working together to sabotage the production. I had figured out what was going on just in the nick of time. The actor was fired and replaced with a friend of mine, Harold Safer, and the film was saved. Today was to be the first day back to production after the whole mess.

"I don't know how relaxing it will be," I said to Dad. "Morris has already lost a lot of time because of the sabotage. It's not going to be easy to finish the movie on budget now."

"I wouldn't worry about that," Dad replied. "Morris Dunnowitz is an experienced producer and director. He'll find a way to cut costs and finish the movie on time."

"Hiring locals like you and Harold helps," Hannah added. "He doesn't have to pay you two the same type of salary that Hollywood actors would demand."

4

A pang of nervousness shot through me again. That was just the problem! Morris, the director, had hired a couple of nonactors to play two of the historically important parts. I didn't know how Mr. Safer felt about it, but I was terrified! Morris had already encountered so many difficulties in trying to make his movie. The last thing I wanted to do was to add to his problems.

The phone rang, making me jump. Dad picked it up. "Drew residence," he said. He listened for a moment, his brow furrowing in concentration. "Sure, Peter," he replied to the caller. "Why don't you come by this afternoon and we can discuss it?"

I took a deep breath and forced myself to finish my waffles as Dad wrapped up the phone call. I had to stop thinking about how nervous I was, because thinking about it only made me more nervous!

"One of your clients?" I asked Dad when he hung up.

He nodded. "A new client, Peter Wyszinski."

I could tell Dad was distracted. Mr. Wyszinski must have given him bad news. "He's the new CFO of Rackham Industries, isn't he?" I asked. I always take an interest in Dad's work. Sometimes I even help his clients solve mysteries of their own.

"That's right," Dad replied.

"Is there some kind of problem?" I asked. I knew

it was a big deal for Dad to be representing Rackham Industries. It was the largest company in the whole city of River Heights. So I was hoping that nothing would go wrong.

"It seems there *is* a problem," Dad told me. "Peter didn't want to discuss it over the phone, so I guess I'll have to wait until this afternoon to find out what it is."

"Finished, Nancy?" Hannah asked, nodding toward my almost-empty plate. I snatched up the last piece of bacon and ate it. "I am now," I said, pushing back my chair. I carried my dirty dishes into the kitchen while Hannah wiped the table. I would have been happy to discuss Dad's new client more, but I was feeling antsy. All of my big scenes were being filmed in the next few days, and I had to be ready.

I ran up to my room, brushed my teeth, slipped on my sneakers, and ran back down to the front door. I was just about to leave when I realized I'd left my car keys on my dresser. With a sigh I headed back up-stairs to get them.

On the way back down, I stuck my head into the dining room. "'Bye, Dad," I said. He glanced up from his coffee. "Break a leg, sweetheart," he told me.

I smiled and continued on to the door. "Nancy, wait!" Hannah cried. "Don't forget your script." She bustled in from the kitchen and handed me the pages I'd left lying on the counter.

"Thanks, Hannah," I said. "I'm forgetting everything this morning." I pulled open the door, but Hannah pushed it closed again.

"There's one more thing you forgot," she said with a grin.

"What?"

Hannah nodded toward the antique mirror that hung in the foyer. One glance showed me that I'd entirely forgotten to brush my hair this morning. It was a mess, with one strawberry blond cowlick standing straight out from my head like an alien's antenna. "Yikes!" I cried, mashing it down.

Hannah chuckled, but I wasn't amused. I couldn't even remember to do the most basic things this morning. How was I ever going to remember my lines for the movie?

2

History or Mystery?

When I got to the production site, I was surprised to discover that I was the first one there. I checked my watch. It was nine o'clock. I checked my call sheet, the piece of paper that listed all the scenes being shot today along with the time that each person was scheduled to arrive. My call time was ten fifteen. I sighed. I'd been so anxious about doing a good job on my scenes that I'd forgotten even to check my own schedule.

I should have called one of my two best friends, Bess Marvin and George Fayne. During the course of my last mystery, I'd gotten both of them jobs here on the movie set. George was in charge of all the computers being used for the production, and Bess ran the construction crew. They both loved their jobs, and, unlike me, they weren't so nervous that they'd forget what time to show up in the morning. But it hadn't occurred to me to check with them, so it looked as if I was on my own until the rest of the crew showed up in an hour or so.

"At least I'll have more time to get into character," I whispered to myself. I was pretty sure I knew my lines, but that didn't mean I'd be able to say them in the way my character would have. If I wanted to be convincing as Esther Rackham, I would have to try to *think* like Esther Rackham.

I made my way over to the trailer I was going to share with Mr. Safer and the two actors playing the Rackham boys, Ben and Luke Alvarez. I knew that on the sets of big Hollywood movies, each actor got his own trailer. The trailer is like a private little living room where actors can go between takes if they want some time alone to prepare for their roles. But this was such a low-budget movie that all the actors had to share trailers in order to save money. I didn't mind. I had known Mr. Safer for years, and I liked the Alvarez brothers.

The door of the trailer was marked with the names of our characters: Esther Rackham, Ethan Mahoney, and John and Ross Rackham. I went inside and sank down onto the tiny couch. There was also a kitchenette, a small table, and a bathroom. It was fine for one person, but if all of us happened to be there at once, we'd have a hard time fitting inside.

I had only been assigned to this trailer since the production started up again after the sabotage. Morris Dunnowitz had closed everything down for four days and worked with the new continuity chief, Kevin Kelley, to reorganize the movie shoot. Kevin and Morris wanted to make sure the entire production was planned around spending as little money as possible.

I pulled out my script and began flipping through it. I knew my own scenes, but I figured that it wouldn't hurt to remind myself of what was happening in the rest of the movie. Morris had given me a crash course in filmmaking when I first began working with him on the movie. One of the things that surprised me is that the scenes of a film aren't shot in the order that they're written. Instead, the scenes are shot according to where they're set. That means that every scene that takes place in a certain location will be filmed on the same day, even if those scenes are supposed to take place days or months apart in the finished movie. By doing this, the film crew saves money. They only have to rent a location for a day or two. Sometimes the crew will build a set inside a big warehouse called a soundstage. That set stays up for as long as it's needed. Usually those sets are the ones that will be used most often.

Since the filming was done out of order, it was difficult to keep track of where in the story my character was. So reading the script from start to finish would help me figure out how Esther would be feeling in my scenes for today.

I flipped through until I reached my favorite part of the story: the part where Ethan Mahoney, the owner of the Mahoney Anvil Company, wakes up in his riverboat office to find that the Rackham boys have set it on fire. They'd knocked Mr. Mahoney unconscious and left him there to die. But Mahoney had the last laugh. He woke up sooner than they'd expected, doused the fire in his office, and tracked the Rackham boys out to a cave by the river. He almost caught them too. Unfortunately he was attacked by a mountain lion inside the cave. The lion mauled him, leaving him too badly injured to walk. He scared off the beast, but had no way to summon help. Out in the wilderness, alone and bleeding, Ethan Mahoney surely would have died if not for my character, Esther Rackham.

Esther's brothers were the ones who had stolen Ethan's money and set his office on fire. So it was especially sweet that Esther was the one to find the ailing Ethan in the cave and save his life. It must have been love at first sight. After he regained his health, Ethan and Esther were married.

11

No one had ever known exactly why Esther happened to be near the cave that day. After she and Ethan married, they lived in seclusion, rarely speaking to anyone. When Esther died, the reason she had been at the cave died with her. In fact, the question of why Esther was there to save Ethan had been one of the first mysteries to intrigue me back when I learned the story in first grade.

Maybe if I try to put myself in Esther's position, I'll be able to figure out how she was feeling that day, I thought. If I can do that, I'll be able to give a terrific performance! I let the script drop onto my lap, put my head back against the couch, and closed my eyes. I tried to imagine how it would feel to be Esther Rackham. What reaction must she have had to finding a badly wounded man out in the middle of nowhere?

Esther's brothers were infamous criminals, two young men known as the Rackham Gang. I was never sure why they were called a gang, since there was just two of them. And criminals or not, Esther must have loved them. Did she know they were going to pull off the heist at the Mahoney Anvil Company? Was she planning to meet them somewhere out near the cave? Or maybe she'd gone there to try to stop them. . . .

I let out a sigh. It was no use. I was supposed to be trying to think of Esther's feelings, and instead I was thinking of the mystery!

"Sleeping on the job, Nancy?" A voice interrupted my thoughts.

I opened my eyes with a start. In the door of my trailer stood Luther Eldridge, the historian Morris Dunnowitz had hired as an advisor on the movie, and a close friend of mine. Luther knew everything about the history of River Heights. He was the perfect person to help Morris make sure the story of the movie was as authentic as possible. And on a personal note, I was thrilled that Luther had agreed to take part in the production. He'd been grieving for years over the loss of his family in a terrible car accident. Ever since they died, Luther had kept to himself, rarely even leaving his house. His daughter, Melissa, had been one of my close friends when we were kids. I still missed her, and I did whatever I could to help out her father. But I wasn't sure that Luther would ever get over his broken heart. It made me smile to see him out and about on the movie set.

"I'm not asleep," I told him. "Just concentrating. I'm trying to make myself feel the way Esther Rackham would've felt."

"Ah," Luther said. "You're becoming a method actor."

I pushed my hair back off my face and looked up at him. "A what?" I asked.

"It's a technique of acting," Luther explained. "It

13

means that you try to apply your own feelings and reactions to the situation that your character is in."

"Well, I don't think it's working," I admitted. "All I can think about is the mystery of Esther Rackham's life."

He nodded. "You may be playing a role in a movie, but you'll always be a detective first," he teased me.

"I know," I said. "But Morris is counting on me. Everyone involved in the film is counting on me. And the production has already been hit with so many problems that I couldn't bear to make it any worse."

Luther studied my face. "You're really worried about this, aren't you?" he asked.

I nodded. "I just can't figure out how to act like Esther."

He sat down next to me. "There's still some time before everyone else gets here. I'd be happy to help you if I can."

"That would be great," I said. "If there's anyone in town who has insight into who Esther Rackham was, it's you."

"I'm not sure even I can be too helpful on that subject," Luther said. "No one knew much about Esther."

"But what about her diary?" I pressed. "In the

script it says that Esther wrote down tons of details every day in her journal."

"It's true. In fact, most of what we know about the River Heist comes from Esther's diary," Luther said. "She was a very detailed writer. She kept track of everything that happened to her from the time she was ten years old."

"Then I can just read her original diary, and she'll tell me *herself* what she was thinking when she went out to that cave!" I said, smiling. I'd heard about Esther's diary before, of course, but I'd never read it. The diary was kept in the town hall in an airtight container to make sure that the old paper didn't disintegrate with time. "Do you think the mayor would give me permission?" I asked. "Or maybe there's a transcript of it somewhere. . . ."

"It wouldn't help," Luther told me. "In fact, I got the mayor's permission to go through the diary again and transcribe it for this movie. Althea came with me. She was fascinated when I told her about the diary." Luther blushed a tiny bit when he mentioned Althea Waters, the screenwriter. I suspected that there might be a romance brewing between Luther and Althea. "At the production meeting today, Althea and I are going to ask Morris to insert a few scenes of Esther writing in her diary," Luther went on. "I think it will make the script much more authentic."

And it would give me even more scenes to perform in. Ugh.

"But the diary doesn't answer your questions," Luther went on. "Because there are no entries for the day when Esther found Ethan Mahoney in the cave, or for the day before that."

I stared at him, surprised. "No entries at all?" I asked, my sleuthing sense on alert. When you've solved as many mysteries as I have, you develop a sort of "sixth sense" about things. And my sixth sense was telling me that a girl who's kept a diary since she was ten doesn't just stop writing the day before a heist by coincidence!

"That's the strange part," Luther said. "It seems as if there were entries at one point, but someone tore them out. There are bits of paper still stuck in the old binding."

Another mystery. "Why would anyone want to tear those pages out?" I asked.

"I don't think we'll ever know," Luther said.

"But she never told anyone what happened to her brothers. They got away!"

"That's true," Luther said. "But there's no reason to think Esther knew where they went. They certainly wouldn't have kept in touch with her once she was married to the man they stole from!"

I smiled. "I guess not."

"And it is thanks to Esther that we know a lot about what happened. For instance, she recorded exactly how much money her brothers stole from Ethan."

"I thought they took *all* his money," I said.

"They took everything he had in his office safe," Luther told me. "There wasn't a bank in the town back in those days; this was still frontier land. Ethan Mahoney kept all his profits right on the premises of the anvil factory."

"So they took all his profits," I said. "But he still had all the anvils. Couldn't he have simply sold them and rebuilt his fortune from the money he made?"

"It was more complicated than that," Luther said. "The money that the Rackham boys took included prepayments for anvils. The railroads were still being built at the time, and Ethan had gotten very large orders for hundreds of anvils. He was paid in advance."

"So when the Rackham Gang took the money, Ethan was left with a bunch of anvils that had already been sold," I said.

"Even worse, he was left with an order for anvils that hadn't been made yet," Luther said. "He had no money left to keep the factory running. He couldn't make any new anvils. His business was bankrupt, and he was never even able to repay the money he'd been given by the railroad company."

"Wow," I said. "I had always heard the story in a way that made it seem as if Ethan Mahoney continued to be a wealthy man even after the River Heist."

"There is some truth to that," Luther admitted. "After Ethan and Esther both died, their heirs were surprised to receive a very large inheritance."

I frowned. "I didn't think they had any kids."

"Ethan had children from his first marriage," Luther explained. "He was a widower when he met Esther."

"She must have really loved him to be willing to marry him even though he was bankrupt," I commented.

"I guess so. Esther stopped writing in her diary after the wedding," Luther said. "And once Ethan had told his story to the local marshal, neither he nor Esther ever spoke of the heist again."

"I imagine it was a strain on their relationship," I said, thinking aloud. "After all, it was Esther's brothers who committed the crime. That can't have been easy on the marriage."

Luther shrugged. "They kept to themselves. They never even let anyone into their house. So nobody knows much about their marriage, or about where the money came from. Ethan's son told people that his father had invested well with what little money he had left after the heist."

That didn't seem quite right to me. If Ethan Mahoney had truly been bankrupt after the River Heist, he couldn't have had very much money to invest. "But the Mahoney family is one of the richest families in River Heights," I said. "Half the buildings in town are named after them."

"That's true," Luther said. "But later generations have added to the amount left by Ethan. And all of the Mahoneys have made a point of giving a lot of money to the city. It's always seemed important to the whole family."

I thought about Mrs. Mahoney, the elderly widow who was one of the last living members of the Mahoney family. She's one of my father's clients, so I know her pretty well. Her husband was notoriously tight fisted with his money, but since his death, Mrs. Mahoney has given away huge amounts to charity. "Well, Mrs. Mahoney certainly thinks it's important," I said. "But her husband didn't."

Luther nodded. "Cornelius Mahoney thought giving away money was a waste of time."

"I have a theory," I said. "I think Mrs. Mahoney donates so much money because she wants people to forget what a nasty guy he was. If there are enough good works done in his name, everyone will think he was a great philanthropist!"

A knock on the trailer door startled me. Janie

Gracen, one of the production assistants, opened the door and stuck her head in. "Excuse me, but Morris wants everyone to meet in the production office before we start shooting for the day," she said.

Luther stood up. "If there's one thing I've learned about moviemaking, it's that when the director calls, everybody listens."

I stayed seated, all my nervousness returning in a rush. "I guess we'd better go," I said, even though I didn't want to do any such thing.

Luther caught my expression. "Don't worry, Nancy, you'll be great," he said. "I've known you since you were a little girl, and I know there's nothing you can't do once you set your mind to it." He gave me a warm smile. "You ready?"

"Sure," I said, getting up. But I knew in my heart that I was nowhere *near* ready. Was I going to ruin the entire movie?

3

A Fiery Start

I hadn't gotten three steps away from the trailer before I felt a hand grab my arm.

"There you are!" cried George, her dark eyes accusing me. "We've been looking all over for you."

"Yeah, we even went by your house to pick you up," her cousin Bess added. "I figured you'd oversleep, as usual."

I mustered a smile for my two best friends. Even though they're related, the two of them couldn't be more different. First, there's the way they look. George is tall and skinny with brown hair that she keeps cut short so it won't get in her way. Bess is shorter and curvy, with long blond hair and sparkling blue eyes. And their personalities are just as different. While George lives for computers and other electronic gadgets, Bess lives for fashion and boys. Or at least that's what you would think if you didn't bother to get to know Bess well. Underneath her girly exterior beats the heart of a die-hard mechanic. She's never met an engine she didn't like. That's why she made the perfect crew chief for the film.

One thing Bess and George *do* have in common, though, is that they both love to tease me!

"Nancy didn't oversleep today," George joked. "It looks like she *under*slept!"

"She's right, Nance," Bess said, pulling a tube of lipstick out of her bag. "You look awful." She held out the lipstick.

"No, thanks," I told her. "The makeup people will just tell me to take it off so they can put their own stuff on me."

"Well, at least tuck your shirt in," Bess said.

I glanced down at my T-shirt to find that one side was tucked into my jeans while the other side hung loose. I tucked the whole thing in. "I forgot to look at the call sheet, so I got here really early," I told them as we all headed toward the production office. "Sorry I made you search all over for me."

"No problem," George said. "I told Bess we should look in your trailer, but she said that was the last place you would be."

"Hey!" Bess retorted. "We're talking about Nancy

22

Drew. I figured she'd be out sniffing up a new mystery, not hiding in her trailer like a movie star."

"Nancy *is* a movie star!" cried Ben Alvarez, coming up behind us. He slung an arm around my shoulders. "She's already saved our movie once with her detective skills—"

"And now she'll save us again with her acting skills," finished his brother, Luke.

The Alvarez brothers were known around the set for being playful. They liked practical jokes, and they liked to tease people. So I knew they were just kidding with me now. Still, I didn't like to hear that anyone was expecting me to save the movie with my acting. It wasn't much of a joke, as far as I was concerned.

"She can't save you if you get fired for being late to the production meeting," Bess teased back.

"Then we'd better hurry," Luke cried. He grabbed her hand and pulled her into a jog.

"Wait for me!" Ben said, running after them.

"See you there!" Bess called to us over her shoulder.

George rolled her eyes good-naturedly. "It's like the Battle of the Flirts," she joked. It was true. No matter what the situation, Bess always finds a boy to flirt with. But the Alvarez brothers were even bigger flirts than she was!

George and I got to the production office just in

time to see Morris Dunnowitz talking with Jake Brigham, the animal wrangler for the film. Jake was in charge of making sure all the animals we used were treated well, and did not get injured.

"I mean it, Morris," I heard Jake say. "I know it's been a struggle, and I'm happy to take less money."

"I appreciate that," Morris replied. "We were on a tight budget to begin with, and I wasn't expecting all the added expenses from Herman Houseman's scheme."

"Of course not," Jake said. "I respect you for wanting to see the movie finished in spite of all that. Most directors would have given up. So I'm willing to take a pay cut."

Morris reached out and shook Jake's hand, and Jake headed into the office.

"Good morning," I said, approaching Morris. He grinned at me. "You don't fool me, Nancy," he said. "I know you were eavesdropping."

"What?" I tried to sound offended.

"Oh, *please,* you know he's right," George teased. "You're always listening to other people's conversations."

"All right. But I can't help it," I defended myself. "It just comes naturally to me after all these years of sleuthing."

"It's okay," Morris said. "If it weren't for your

24

detective work, we wouldn't have a movie to make." He pulled open the door to the office and held it for George and me.

"It's really nice of Jake to take a pay cut," I said, stepping into the main production office. This was Morris's headquarters, where all the producers and editors had their offices. A large group of people was already gathered around the common area, and were sitting on chairs, desks, and the floor.

"You'd be surprised about how many people have offered to take less money," Morris said quietly. "It's as if Herman Houseman's sabotage efforts just brought everyone else together. They all want to see this movie get made, even if they don't get paid for it." He glanced around at all the smiling, excited faces. "Look, Nancy. They're all thrilled to be here, and it's thanks to you."

My heart sank. Everyone certainly did look happy. It was a big change from when we'd last had a production meeting, before I uncovered Herman Houseman's sabotage scheme. Back then, everyone was miserable. That's because there had been so many mishaps on set that most people thought the movie was cursed. People had been grumbling and unhappy and ready to quit. But now they were all smiles. I could feel the excitement crackling in the air.

But I didn't share their mood. I was too nervous

about the scenes I'd be filming later in the day.

"Okay, everybody," Morris called over the din. "Let's make this a quick meeting. I'm sure we all want to get back out there and start shooting."

The cast and crew hooted and hollered their agreement.

"So here's the plan," Morris went on. "We're going right back to the beginning. We'll re-film all the scenes we shot with Houseman—"

The group broke into hisses and boos upon hearing the old actor's name.

"With our new star, River Heights's own Harold Safer," Morris finished.

I joined in the clapping as Mr. Safer stepped up to stand beside Morris. As far as I was concerned, Mr. Safer was born to play the role of Ethan Mahoney. He's naturally dramatic, whether he's describing the latest sunset he's seen, or the latest Broadway play. Mr. Safer owns the cheese shop in town, but his true love has always been the theater. I felt sure that he must have picked up some acting skills over his years of watching other people act.

"So today we'll start with the scenes that take place in Ethan Mahoney's office," Morris said. "First we'll do Ethan at work, which is a quick scene. Next, we'll go to the Rackham boys breaking in and fighting with Ethan. And after that we'll do the scene where the Rackham boys and Esther visit the anvil office to case the joint. Let's get to work."

Everyone scattered as I went over the shot list in my mind. My scene was going to be filmed third. Good. That still gave me some time before I had to get ready.

"Hey, do you guys want to grab a snack over at the mess hall?" I asked Bess and George. The mess hall was a temporary building made of metal. Inside was the craft table, where the caterers set up breakfast, lunch, and dinner, and set out snacks all day. The idea was to keep everyone on set so they could eat as quickly as possible and get back to work. If they had to leave the production camp and drive to a restaurant in town, lunch hour would become lunch *two* hours.

"No, thanks," George said. "I had to help Mom stuff all that food into the car this morning. I never want to even smell another spinach quiche again. It took forty minutes to get it all packed."

I knew I should take George's complaint with a grain of salt. Really, she was thrilled when she got her mother's catering company hired to make all the food for the shoot. The old caterer had been fired after a big food-poisoning incident—one more example of Herman Houseman's sabotage.

"Count me out too. I have to get over to the

Rackhams' cabin set," Bess said. "As soon as they finish the office scenes, they're going to move on to the cabin scenes. And I still haven't finished fixing the slanty wall on that set."

Before I knew it, my friends had hurried off to their jobs, leaving me alone with my stage fright. Harold Safer walked toward me, a plaid robe covering his Ethan Mahoney costume. He looked kind of silly, but I had gotten used to seeing people in robes. The costumers paid so much attention to every smudge of dirt and loose button on the clothes, and they didn't want anything to ruin the effect. Even something as simple as walking twenty yards from a trailer to a set could damage the costume. So we all wore robes over our costumes to protect them.

"Wish me luck, Nancy," he said once he was close. "I've never acted before."

"Break a leg, Mr. Safer," I told him.

"Please, Nancy—we've been friends for a while. Call me Harold."

He gave me a huge smile and hurried toward the soundstage. Now why couldn't I be more like him, cool and composed? Harold and I were in the same situation; neither of us had any experience as actors, and both of us had roles in the movie. But when I was afraid, he was excited.

What was his secret? I decided to follow him. I

had a while before my scenes. I thought maybe it would ease my mind to watch Harold's introduction to the acting world.

When I got to the soundstage, one of the production assistants was just about to close the door. I just made it into the darkness inside. The soundstage was a big empty warehouse that had been turned into a movie set. The two locations constructed here were called standing sets. That meant that these sets stayed up throughout the duration of the shoot. When filming took place "on location"—out in actual buildings and places around River Heights—the construction crew built a set around whatever was there already. Then, when we were done filming, the crew tore down everything they had built, leaving the place just as they had found it. But the sets for the places we were going to use the most, the Mahoney Anvil office and the Rackham Gang's cabin, had been created here, inside the soundstage. It was pretty impressive. Every time I walked into either place, I felt as if I was in a real building. Every last detail was perfect.

When the crew was filming a scene, everyone inside the giant warehouse had to be completely silent. The sophisticated microphones used by the sound crew could pick up even the smallest noise. So whenever the director called "Action," everyone stopped what they were doing and waited until they heard "Cut!" In the time in between, no one was allowed to talk. In fact, people weren't even allowed to walk because their footsteps might echo too loudly inside the big building. I had just enough time to make it to the Mahoney Anvil office set before I heard Morris's distinctive, gravelly voice yell, "Mahoney work scene, take one. Action!"

I caught my breath, afraid to move. What if I knocked into something or stumbled over one of the thick electrical cables on the floor? I've been known to be a klutz from time to time. But soon enough my fear of making noise was forgotten. I couldn't think of anything except how amazing Harold was! He was a natural. I'd seen this scene before, when it was shot with the famous Herman Houseman in the role. And Harold Safer was better!

From the second the scene began, he seemed like a different person. His usual nervous mannerisms were gone. He walked with a swagger and he spoke with the booming, commanding voice of a man who created an empire out of making anvils. I was looking at Harold's familiar face, but all I saw was Ethan Mahoney.

Without moving, I took a look around at all the other people watching. There were at least twenty people standing nearby—all the camera and sound crew members, the makeup and hair people, an assistant director, and lots of production assistants. And on each face I saw the same astonished expression. No-body had expected it, but Harold was a terrific actor.

"That payment had better be here in two days," Harold–as–Ethan said, ending the scene.

"And . . . cut!" Morris called.

Instantly the whole group burst into applause. Even Morris was clapping. Harold looked confused for a moment, until he realized the cheering was for him. He took a deep, theatrical bow.

"That was wonderful," Morris said when the clapping died down. "Now we'll do another take so we can shoot close-ups of your expressions, Harold. Everyone, back to your first marks."

Harold and the other actors hurried back to where they were supposed to stand at the beginning of the scene. "Action," called Morris.

The scene began again, and it was every bit as good as the first time. I wished George and Bess were here to see Harold's triumph. I was so wrapped up in the scene that I didn't notice Julie Blattberg, the sound chief, leave her post at the giant sound board. But suddenly I spotted her pushing her way toward Morris. She lifted one of his earphones and said something to him.

"Cut!" Morris yelled immediately.

The camera operators stopped filming and the actors relaxed. Everyone looked at Morris to see why he'd made them pause, but I already knew. As soon as the actors had stopped talking, I'd heard sirens wailing in the distance. They weren't very loud, but I knew that Julie had caught them. She must have been worried that the microphones would pick up the sound, and sirens like those would be completely out of place in a movie that was set almost a hundred years ago.

"Let's wait for the sirens to pass," Julie called out.

The makeup artist, Pam, rushed over to Harold and began powdering his face while her associate, a muscular guy named Degas, smoothed down a few strands of Harold's thick dark hair. I smiled. Harold obviously loved all the attention.

A second siren joined the first one. I stepped away from the small crowd around the set and listened more closely. The sirens droned on, each of them giving a little *whoop* before starting up again. "It's not the police, it's the fire squad," I whispered. The sirens were similar, but I had a knack for noticing little details. And I definitely knew the difference between police sirens and fire sirens.

A third siren joined in. I gasped in surprise. *Three* fire trucks?

I glanced over at Harold Safer, the only other River Heights local on the set. He didn't look happy anymore; he looked worried. His gaze met mine.

"Must be a pretty big fire," he said in a worried tone. I knew what he was thinking. He was worried about his cheese shop and his house. Now that I thought about it, I was worried about *my* house too. From inside this windowless building, it was impossible to tell what direction the sirens were coming from. They could be in any neighborhood in town. It could be Harold's business on fire. Or George's house. Or Bess's.

Or mine.

4

Burning Down the House

The sirens stopped after another minute or two, but my nervousness continued. Morris called for everyone to start the scene one more time. As the camera operators and the actors scrambled back to their first marks, I took advantage of the noise and confusion to slip out of the soundstage before he ordered quiet again. The delay in filming meant my scene wouldn't begin shooting for a bit longer than we'd originally planned. I would have time to go into town and check out the fire.

I was anxious to discover where the blaze was, to make sure none of my friends' houses were in danger. And I thought getting away from the set might ease my stage fright. If I had something else to think about, I wouldn't be able to spend all my time worrying.

I decided to see if Bess or George wanted to come with me. I knew George was going to be in the editing trailer this morning, working on one of the giant computers that the editors used to process the shots. I headed that way, knocked on the trailer door, and let myself in.

"George?" I called. "Do you have time to investigate the fire with me?"

Right away I knew the answer was no. George was working three computers at once—two laptops, and the big editing machine. I'm pretty good at figuring out how to solve my own basic computer problems, and I can find a lot of stuff online, but George is a true wiz. Once she gets going on a computer problem, her fingers fly across the keyboard and pump out computer language so fast that I can't even figure out what she's doing half the time.

This time, she didn't even hear me. "George?" I repeated.

She glanced up and gave me a fast smile. "Hey, Nance," she said. "What's up?"

"I'm going to take a drive and see where the fire is," I told her.

But George's eyes had already returned to the screen of the big computer. "What fire?" she mumbled.

"The one that had at least three fire engines rushing to put it out," I said. "Didn't you hear all those sirens?"

"Uh, no," George said slowly. I could tell that her attention was focused on the computers, not our conversation. She probably didn't even know what she was saying no to!

"Well, it's a big fire," I went on. "I'm going to take a drive and make sure it's not at any of our houses. I think I'll run past Harold's cheese shop too. That way I can set his mind at ease so he can concentrate on his acting."

"Okay, have fun," George said. I couldn't help a smile. She really hadn't heard a word I'd said.

"See you later," I told her. But George wasn't even pretending to listen anymore. She was completely wrapped up in solving her computer problems. It was time to try Bess.

I found her in the second soundstage, working on the Rackhams' cabin set. She was perched high up on a ladder as Luther Eldridge called out instructions. I walked over to join him.

"What's going on?" I asked.

"Oh, Nancy, it's a disaster!" he cried. "When Bess removed the molding around the top of the walls, we discovered that whoever built this set didn't put anything behind the moldings."

I glanced around. The cabin set looked just like a real cabin, except that it didn't have a roof. On one side Bess had taken down the molding at the top of the wall. Now that wall was about five inches shorter than it had been with the molding. It looked ridiculous. With the carved wooden molding, the walls had given the illusion that there was a ceiling. On camera the room would look like a regular, finished cabin. But now, with the short walls, it would look more like a child's play fort.

"It looks like we'll have to put the molding back up," I said.

"But we can't!" Luther sounded horrified. "A rustic nineteenth-century cabin wouldn't have such things. Carved moldings were for the large houses of wealthy people."

I took a look at Bess. Her cheeks were smudged with dirt, and her jeans and T-shirt were covered in sawdust, but there was a determined gleam in her eyes. "We'll figure something out," she said confidently.

Clearly this was not the time to ask Bess to come for a drive with me. "Well, good luck, you two," I said, backing out of the set.

I was on my own. I made my way to the car and started the ten-minute drive into River Heights. To my surprise, I didn't even see smoke. I drove through the center of town and glanced at Harold's cheese shop. It was fine. So were all the other shops and offices nearby. I continued on to my neighborhood, then drove past George's house, and Bess's. There was no fire to be seen.

There was only one place I hadn't looked yet—Mission Hill. That's the neighborhood that puts the "heights" in River Heights. The hill rises high over the town, and from the top there are amazing views of the Muskoka River. It's the most expensive area in the whole city. I started up the winding road that led to the top of the hill. Immediately I could tell I was on the right trail.

Police cars and fire trucks lined the side of the road, and thick brown smoke wafted through the air. The houses in this neighborhood were set far back from the road, and each place was surrounded by a lot of property. I found the flaming house about half a mile from the top of the hill. It was a beautiful old Georgian-style house with tall columns in front of the entrance. And it was being devoured by angry orange flames that leaped high into the sky. Heavy smoke poured from the fire, billowing across the manicured front lawn.

I pulled my car to the side of the street and got out. Three separate teams of firefighters held their powerful hoses on the blaze, but the water didn't seem to be doing much good.

River Heights Fire Chief Cody Cloud stood near the curb, commanding his firefighters through the walkie-talkie in his hand. He frowned when he saw me.

"Nancy, what are you doing here?" he asked.

"Hi, Chief Cody," I said. "We heard the sirens on the set and I thought I'd take a drive out just to make sure the fire wasn't at any of our houses."

"No, the owner of this house isn't involved in your film," Chief Cody said. He pointed out a middle-aged man on the front lawn. The man was racing back and forth in front of the burning house, panicked.

From the way the owner was acting, I assumed he was worried about a family member who hadn't escaped the fire. "Is there someone else inside?" I asked Chief Cody.

"Nope," he said. "That guy lives here alone. He's worried about his stuff."

At that moment the owner gave up on his pacing and ran over to where we were standing. "Aren't you in charge here?" he demanded.

Chief Cody nodded. "We're doing everything we can, Jeffrey," he said in a soothing voice.

"It's not enough," Jeffrey snapped. "All of my furniture is going to be ruined."

"We're fighting to save your house," Chief Cody explained. "The furniture can be replaced."

"No, it can't!" Jeffrey cried, distraught. "Don't you

get it? The house is filled with antique furniture. I put all my money into the furniture collection. If it's destroyed, I'll be ruined. I'll be destitute!"

"Now, Jeffrey—," the fire chief began.

"They're spraying water into the house!" Jeffrey shrieked, pointing to a team of firefighters who had just turned their hoses toward the one part of the house that wasn't burning.

"They're wetting everything down to try to keep the fire from spreading," Chief Cody explained.

But Jeffrey seemed even more agitated than before. "Water will ruin my furniture just as much as fire will!" he cried.

I could tell Chief Cody was losing patience with this owner. After all, his firefighters were putting themselves in danger trying to save the house, and Jeffrey didn't seem grateful at all.

"Maybe that team can stop wetting things down and just concentrate on getting some of the furniture out?" I suggested.

Jeffrey looked at me, noticing me for the first time. His mouth opened and closed, but he didn't say anything.

"That would mean sending firefighters into a burning building," Chief Cody replied. "It's a dangerous thing to do. We go inside to save people and animals, but not to save furniture."

"The room over there isn't on fire," I said, gesturing to what looked like a large hall or living room. It stuck out from the main structure, as if it had been added on after the house was built. "And the wind is blowing the other way. I'll bet some of the firefighters could get the furniture out of there without the fire spreading to them."

Chief Cody shot Jeffrey an annoyed look. "I guess we might as well try," he said. He turned away and began barking orders to his team through the walkie-talkie.

"I'm so sorry about your house," I told Jeffrey. "How did the fire start?" He gazed at me blankly. I figured he was probably in shock. "I'm Nancy Drew," I added. "I'd like to help in any way I can."

"Th-Thank you," he stammered.

"Here's a piece," called one of the firefighters. Jeffrey turned and ran toward the large armoire that two men had just lugged from the house. It was badly damaged by the smoke and heat, but still in good enough condition that it could be restored to its original state. I felt a little bit better looking at it—at least Jeffrey wouldn't lose *all* of his antique collection.

But he acted as if it was burned beyond recognition. "It's ruined!" he cried. "Utterly destroyed!" Jeffrey threw his arms around the armoire in a dramatic

41

gesture. I noticed him plucking at something on the back of it as he embraced the piece of furniture.

"Get out. Get out now," I heard Chief Cody command. I looked back at the house to see that the wind had changed. The dark smoke that had been blowing away from the addition had begun blowing in the opposite direction. Clouds of toxic smoke and smoldering embers were now billowing right onto the one part of the house that had seemed safe.

I glanced over at Jeffrey. The poor guy had the worst luck in the world. It didn't look like they'd be able to save any more of his valuable furniture. The two firefighters who had carried the armoire came running back out of the house just as a spark hit the roof of the addition and set it aflame. One of them went over to Jeffrey and handed him a laptop computer.

"I was able to grab this," the firefighter said. "Sorry we couldn't save more."

Jeffrey took the computer and looked at it for a moment. Then he hurled it back toward the burning house with a bellow of anger. "It's useless!" he cried. "This is all useless!" He stormed off toward a black SUV parked in the driveway. He got in and peeled out without saying another word.

I shot a look at Chief Cody to see how he was handling Jeffrey's anger. But the chief was busy organizing a plan to keep the fire from spreading to the nearby trees and houses. He stood surrounded by about five firefighters.

The house was still in the midst of bright orange flames that leaped into the sky. I could tell that the entire place would be destroyed. My eyes were beginning to sting from all the heat and smoke. It was time for me to leave. But as I turned to go, I realized that something was nagging at the back of my mind. What had Jeffrey been plucking at on the back of his armoire?

The chief and his colleagues were still huddled together. No one was paying any attention to me. So I pulled the collar of my shirt up over my mouth and nose to block out the smoke. Then I took a few steps toward the house, and the armoire, which had been abandoned on the front lawn. I ducked behind the large chest to see if I could find anything on the back. To my surprise, the back of the armoire was an entirely different color from the front. The piece had appeared to be made of rich reddish cherrywood. But the back was beige and made of pressed wood— usually the mark of less expensive furniture. And right in the middle of the pressed wood was a big sticker that read O'REILLY BROS.

I frowned and leaned in closer. The edges of the sticker were singed and the smoke had blackened the lettering. But I could still read it. "O'Reilly Brothers furniture?" I murmured. "How odd."

O'Reilly Bros. is a big store on the outskirts of town. They sell cheap furniture, the kind that's made of particle board—in other words, not real wood. The pieces are covered by a thin panel of stained wood so that the furniture looks nice. Usually the kind of people who buy furniture from O'Reilly Bros. are young married couples just moving into their first home, or college kids looking for cheap dorm room furnishings. Definitely not rich guys who live in mansions up in the Mission Hill neighborhood.

But Jeffrey had thrown his arms around this armoire as if it was one of his prized antiques. Could he have been confused and mistaken it for a more valuable piece? Or did this particular armoire have sentimental value for some reason? There had to be some explanation for why a wealthy man who collected antique furniture would have a cheap piece like this.

"I'm going to need you to move back, Nancy," Chief Cody said, striding up to me. "You're too close to the fire. A spark might catch your hair or your clothes."

"Sorry, Chief," I replied. "I'll get out of your way."

I hurried toward my car, fighting to breathe in the

smoky air. At the end of the driveway I spotted a mailbox that I hadn't seen on the way in. When I saw the name on the side, I gasped.

"Allman," I read aloud. "That was Jeffrey Allman!" He was the man who had recently retired as the CFO of Rackham Industries. My father and I had been talking about him only this morning.

I shuddered. It was terrible to think of a retiree losing his whole house and all his money. Poor Jeffrey Allman. Compared to his troubles, my stage fright problem seemed completely silly. I started up the car and pulled out. I could hardly wait to get back to the set. After the sad reality of the fire, a little moviemaking glamour would be welcome.

5

The Natural

The instant I set foot in the makeup trailer, Pam and Degas pounced on me.

"I was about to send out a search party!" Degas joked. He spun the makeup chair around and gestured for me to sit.

"We only have ten minutes to transform you into Esther," Pam said. "We're lucky you look so much like her to begin with!" It was true. One of the reasons Morris had asked me to play the Rackhams' sister was because I happen to resemble the old photos of Esther.

Degas pulled my hair back into a tight ponytail and began forming it into a proper nineteenth-century bun. Pam whipped out my makeup chart. It listed everything she needed to use on my face to make me into Esther. Before production shut down due to Herman Houseman's sabotage, these two had spent hours experimenting with makeup on me. Now I could understand why they'd done such an in-depth job. Because they'd figured out what to do back then, they now had a list of everything that was needed. It was as if they had a blueprint of my face; all they had to do was follow their directions, and I'd become Esther Rackham.

Before I knew it, I was made up and on my way to the wardrobe trailer. It was the same story there. I stepped inside, and within five minutes Julie Wilson, the wardrobe assistant, had me costumed in Esther's long dress.

As I wrapped myself in a robe to keep the dress clean, Luke Alvarez knocked on the trailer door.

"Is Nancy here?" he asked, sticking his head in.

"I don't know about Nancy, but Esther Rackham is here," Julie teased.

Luke looked me up and down and whistled. "If you weren't my sister, I'd want to ask you on a date," he said.

"Even with this ugly bun?" I asked, putting a hand up to my hair. I wasn't used to such severe styles. Usually I just let my shoulder-length hair fall loose around my face.

Before Luke could answer, his brother Ben called from outside. "We're late!"

Luke rolled his eyes. "Sorry, Nancy," he said. "But Ben and I have been sent to find you. Morris wants to get started on our scene. It's the last one of the day, and everyone is anxious to get it over with and go home."

"I'm ready," I said, tying the robe closed. With a wave to Julie, I stepped outside. Luke offered me his arm, and so did Ben. I took them both, and the boys practically carried me between them over to the soundstage. They teased me the whole way, making fun of my hair and my ugly black button-up boots. As an only child, I'm not used to being ribbed like that. They were acting exactly how I imagined *real* big brothers would act, and I liked it!

By the time we got to the set, I was having a blast. The scene we were about to film was one in which the whole Rackham family visited the Mahoney Anvil office. Esther thought they were there to buy an anvil for her brothers to use in their new blacksmithing business, but the Rackham boys were really there to check out the office. They were already plotting their heist, and they needed to see exactly where in the office Ethan Mahoney's safe was so that they could plan their break-in.

The whole scene took place while the Rackhams were waiting in the office for Ethan to come in. It was just me and the Alvarez brothers. Harold Safer was finished filming for the day, but he was still there on set. He came over as soon as I arrived.

"Nancy, you look terrific!" he cried.

"Thanks, Harold," I said. "I found the fire, by the way. Your house and the cheese shop are both safe."

"Oh, thank goodness." He mopped his brow. "This acting job is a lot of fun, but I don't think it's going to turn into a whole career. If anything happened to the cheese shop, I'd be doomed."

"I don't know about that," Ben Alvarez interrupted. "You're a natural actor, Harold. You may have to move to Hollywood after this!"

At that, Harold blushed bright red.

"Speaking of natural actors," Morris Dunnowitz interrupted, coming over to us, "let's get Miss Nancy Drew in front of the cameras."

"Break a leg, Nancy," Harold said. "I'll be cheering you on from the sidelines."

"Oh, Harold, you must be exhausted," I replied. "You don't have to stay to watch me."

"I wouldn't miss it for the world," he said.

"Neither would we!" added Bess. I turned to see George and Bess hurrying in before the soundstage door was closed.

My heart gave a jump. All my friends on the set were going to be watching? Chills shot down my spine. I'd managed to forget my fear while goofing around with the Alvarez brothers, but now it was returning full force.

I didn't have time to focus on my fears, though, because Morris quickly ushered us all onto the set. A production assistant was busy snapping instant photos of the Mahoney Anvil office. As soon as the photos developed, the set dresser, Mary Lupiani, compared them to instant photos taken when the set was first designed. Before any footage could be shot, Mary had to make sure that every prop and every bit of furniture was in exactly the right place. She and her assistants checked every set before every take. It was the only way to make sure the film footage was consistent. I knew that they had to do this, because when the editors sat down to put the movie together, they would use shots from many different takes. When you watch a scene in a movie, you might be watching one actor talking during one take, and another actor reacting during an entirely different take. The editing machines piece everything together seamlessly, but if even one prop changes place from one take to the next, the entire take is useless.

Once Mary gave us the go-ahead, Morris called, "Action!"

I stood rooted to the ground in horror. I had expected a rehearsal first—that's the way Morris usually did it. He was probably in a real rush to finish. But I wasn't prepared. Ever since I'd gotten back from the fire at Jeffrey Allman's house, everything had happened so quickly. I hadn't even had time to go over my lines for the scene. In fact, I could barely remember whether I *had* lines in this scene!

Luckily Ben and Luke Alvarez knew just what they were doing. They prowled around the office, looking in every cabinet. They were acting as Ross and John Rackham, looking for the office safe. I just stood there, watching them in confusion until I remembered what I was supposed to do.

"Mr. Mahoney will be here any minute," I said, frowning as I tried to remember my lines. "You two had best stop your nosing around."

Ben, as Ross Rackham, laughed. "Calm down, Sissy," he said. "We're just curious." He came over and helped me into one of the office chairs. While he distracted me, Luke, as John Rackham, pulled aside a painting of a sunset to reveal an old-fashioned safe.

"And . . . cut!" Morris called.

I heard applause and cheers from my friends, but my head was still spinning. Morris came onto the set to talk to us while the production assistants moved the painting back over the safe. "Ben, I'd like you to sound a bit more guilty when you talk to Esther," Morris said. "You're lying to your little sister, after all."

Ben nodded.

Then Morris turned to me. "Nancy, you were

perfect," he gushed. "The confusion on your face was completely real."

No wonder why! Lucky for me, my stage fright worked in my favor—Esther is *supposed* to be confused in this scene. She has no idea why her brothers are snooping around the office, and she's baffled by their behavior.

I took a deep breath, trying to calm my nerves. I had gotten through that take, but it wasn't because I did a good acting job. I happened to be feeling the way my character was feeling. But in the next take, I was going to have to *act*. I didn't think I could do it.

"Action!" Morris called.

Somehow I managed to stumble through two more takes. Morris didn't give me any more compliments—he focused mainly on the Alvarez brothers, since they were the real stars of the movie.

By the time I had changed back into my regular clothes to go home, my heartbeat had slowed a tiny bit. The nervousness had been replaced by embarrassment. Morris and the Alvarez boys had told me that I did a good job, but I couldn't help wondering if they were only saying that to be polite. I was convinced that I had made a fool of myself.

When I went down to the dining room for dinner that night, my dad greeted me with a big smile. "There's my favorite actress," he teased.

I knew what *that* meant. He was going to ask me all about my day on the set, but that was the last thing I wanted to talk about. Time to change the subject.

"Hi, Dad," I said. I sat down at my place across from him. "How did your meeting with Peter Wyszinski go?"

It worked like a charm. Dad's face grew serious, and I could see that my adventures in acting were forgotten. "It was pretty disturbing, actually," he said. "Peter hasn't even been the CFO of Rackham Industries for a month, and already he's running into major trouble."

I frowned. "What sort of trouble?" Usually I wouldn't give much thought to the worries of corporate bigwigs, but Rackham Industries is the biggest company in River Heights. They employ more people and create more city revenue than anyone else. If Rackham Industries was in trouble, it meant that all of River Heights was in trouble.

"Accounting problems," Dad said.

I wrinkled my nose. That sounded boring. "You mean their accountants messed up?"

Dad shook his head. "No, I mean someone has been cooking their books," he said grimly.

I gasped. "Mr. Wyszinski thinks the accounts have been purposely falsified? Who would do something like that?"

Dad shrugged. "Any number of people could have done it. The big problem is that there's no proof. All of this happened before Peter took over as CEO. He doesn't even know if the books have been altered to hide some kind of overspending by the company, or if it's a simple case of embezzling."

"Then how does he know there's a problem?" I asked.

"The numbers just don't make sense," Dad told me. "He's got a new team of accountants looking into it. But that's still not going to give him any hard evidence."

I smelled a rat. "And if there was hard evidence, I bet it all went up in smoke just today," I said.

"What do you mean?"

"That big three-alarm fire was at the home of Jeffrey Allman," I told my father. "Didn't you say he just retired from being the CFO at Rackham?"

Dad nodded, his eyebrows knit together in concern. "I heard the sirens, but I had no idea the fire was at Jeffrey's house."

I filled him in on my visit to the Allman house that afternoon. "And I drove by again on my way home from the set," I added. "There was just a pile of ashes left. I'll bet the only thing that survived was the armoire I saw."

"Was it still there?" Dad asked.

I shook my head. "They must have hauled it away.

What a shame that the only thing they managed to save didn't even have any value."

Dad was still frowning. "I've known Jeffrey for years," he murmured. "I didn't know he collected antique furniture."

"I didn't know you were friends with him," I said.

"Oh, we're just very casual acquaintances," Dad replied. "We'd see each other at the occasional town council meeting."

The doorbell rang, interrupting our conversation. Hannah answered it, and a moment later she showed Bess and George into the dining room.

Bess's hand flew to her mouth when she saw us at the table. "Oh, sorry!" she cried. "We thought you'd be finished with dinner by now."

"Don't worry about it," Dad said. "We're eating late because Nancy had a long day on the set."

"Why don't you girls sit down and have some dessert?" Hannah asked, bustling in with two extra plates. "I made my famous caramel cheesecake."

George sat down immediately. "No need to ask me twice," she joked.

Bess took a seat next to her. "Did you hear all about Nancy's triumph?" she asked my father.

My heart sank. I'd been hoping to avoid talking about my acting. In fact, I'd been hoping to avoid even *thinking* about it tonight.

"No, I didn't," Dad said. "How was she?"

"She's a star," George said. "She and Harold were both great!"

"Well, *Harold* was great," I agreed. "I only had one tiny scene to do today, and I managed to mess it up. I couldn't remember my line."

"Don't believe her, Mr. Drew," Bess said. "She was terrific. The director said she looked completely natural."

"That's just because I got lucky—"

George cut me off with a snort. "Here comes the famous Nancy Drew modesty," she teased. My father and Bess both laughed.

"Nancy is the talk of the set," Bess reported. "The carpenters on my team were saying that she's going to have to give up solving mysteries and focus on her acting full-time."

I looked at my friends' smiling faces. I'd been hoping to confide in them about my jitters, but now it was clear to me that they would never understand. Even when I admitted that I had done a bad job, they thought I was just being modest. How could I get them to believe that I had serious doubts about my acting abilities? I sighed. I'd have to deal with the stage fright on my own.

"So did you ever get to that fire, Nance?" George asked.

I nodded, relieved by the change of subject. "I was just telling Dad about it. The place belonged to Jeffrey Allman, the former CFO of Rackham Industries."

"And if you ask me, the fire seems a little suspicious," Dad put in. "Whoever was monkeying with the accounts at Rackham Industries would have a motive for getting rid of evidence. And there might be evidence at the home of the old CFO."

"So you think it might have been arson?" Bess asked.

I shrugged. "Mr. Allman certainly seemed devastated. He claimed that he'd be ruined if the house burned down because all his money had been invested in his antique furniture collection."

George whistled. "Did they manage to save any of it?"

"Nothing," I said. "Well, except for an armoire from O'Reilly Brothers."

"That's weird," George said bluntly. "Why would he have cheap furniture from a place like that mixed in with his antiques?"

"Maybe he really needed an armoire, but he'd spent all his money on antiques," Bess said.

"That's possible," I agreed. "He acted as if it was a valuable piece, though. I guess it could have had sentimental value."

"And that's the only thing they could save from the whole house?" George asked.

"They only had a few minutes inside before the last room caught fire," I said. "One of the firefighters rescued a laptop computer, but Mr. Allman was so agitated and angry that he threw it back into the fire."

All the blood left George's face. "He threw his computer into the fire?" she cried.

Even though the subject was so serious, I couldn't help smiling at George's reaction. To a computer lover like her, purposely harming a laptop probably seemed like the worst possible crime.

"He was so upset," I explained. "I think he threw the computer because he was frustrated."

"But he could have salvaged some of the information on it," George said. "I mean, furniture can be replaced, but who *knows* if he'll be able to recover any files from his hard drive. That laptop may have been his only chance!"

Bess rolled her eyes. "He wasn't worried about the computer, George," she pointed out. "You may *think* the furniture can be replaced, but he obviously didn't."

Still, George did have a point. Since everything else in the house was gone, it was unlikely that any of Jeffrey Allman's files had survived. The computer probably contained at least a few valuable documents.

"Did he throw it all the way into the fire?" George asked.

"I don't think so," I said. "He threw it toward the fire, but it can't have gone all the way back into the house. I think it probably just landed on the lawn."

George pushed back her chair. "Let's go look."

Bess pulled her car to a stop in front of the remains of the Allman house. She gave a low whistle. "This must have been one expensive house," she said.

"It was," I agreed. "A big Georgian-style place. It was almost a mansion."

George opened the back door and climbed out. "Hard to believe the whole thing is gone," she said as Bess and I joined her on the sidewalk.

"There's police tape," Bess pointed out. The yellow tape was strung around what was left of the lawn.

"I'm sure the fire department considers this a possible crime scene," I said. "If Dad and I both found the fire suspicious, it's a good guess that Chief Cody did too."

George squinted into the darkness. The dark shadow that had been the house was lit only by the nearby streetlamps. I pulled out the little flashlight I always keep in my purse and trained the thin beam of light onto the wreckage. I could pick out the brick chimneys of three fireplaces standing up from the ashes like lonely sentinels. The rest of the house was nothing but rubble.

Suddenly George gasped. She grabbed my hand and pointed the flashlight at a spot on the blackened grass. "There's the laptop!" she exclaimed.

Before I knew it, she had ducked under the police tape and was heading for the computer.

"George!" Bess cried. "Get back here!"

But George ignored her. She crunched across the burned grass and picked up the laptop.

"This is a possible crime scene," I called, trying to keep my voice low. "You can't take that!"

George gave me a defiant look. "It's not like the computer is worth anything," she said. "And we know it had nothing to do with starting the blaze. You said yourself that they got the laptop from the room that was last to catch fire."

I bit my lip. She had a point. But I wasn't comfortable removing evidence—any evidence. "We're still not allowed to take it," I protested weakly.

George tucked the burned-out computer under her arm and marched back over to us. "Not many people would be able to salvage anything from this computer," she said. "But I might be able to find something left on the hard drive. Don't you think that would comfort Mr. Allman?"

I exchanged a look with Bess. "I guess it might make him feel a tiny bit better," Bess said.

I sighed. "Oh, all right," I mumbled.

With a triumphant grin George led the way back to the car.

I shook my head and followed her. I had to admit, a part of me felt better knowing that she'd be looking into the computer. I didn't know what I expected her to find, but it was a good thing that someone was digging for details about Jeffrey Allman's house.

Because honestly, something about that fire just didn't sit right with me. I had a hunch that it was more than an accidental blaze. And I'm a girl who's used to believing in her hunches.

6

The Long, Bad Day

Action!" Morris yelled.

I jumped, surprised. I hadn't even realized that we were ready to start shooting. I felt a moment of panic as I realized that I'd forgotten to go to the makeup trailer this morning. My face was bare, and my hair was just lying like it usually did. Not only that, but I was still wearing my pajamas, which were flannel with pictures of teapots on them. Why had they let me on the set looking like this?

I glanced up to see Ben and Luke Alvarez staring at me, waiting for my line.

I opened my mouth, but my mind was a complete blank. I couldn't even remember what scene we were shooting.

"I said *action*," Morris bellowed.

Luke rolled his eyes. "Look at her," he said to his brother. "She's completely unprepared."

Ben nodded. "I knew Morris should have gotten a real actress to play this part. Nancy Drew is such an amateur."

Harold Safer stepped onto the set. "Not only is she an amateur, but she's utterly talentless," he said with a sniff.

I couldn't believe it! Harold was supposed to be my friend. I'd helped him out of a lot of jams, and I'd solved mysteries for him. I was just beginning to feel comfortable calling him by his first name occasionally. "Um, you're an amateur too," I pointed out.

He laughed. "Yes, I am. But I'm actually *good* at acting. You're only here because Morris felt sorry for you."

I felt the blood rush to my cheeks as I blushed. I had never been so mortified in my entire life!

"I don't feel sorry for her anymore," Morris called. "She's fired! She's ruining the whole movie!"

Everyone in the crew began clapping and cheering. Harold pursed his lips and made a strange buzzing sound. The buzzing grew louder and louder, until I finally realized that it was my alarm clock.

I sat up in bed, my cheeks still hot from embarrassment. It had only been a dream. But I couldn't shake the feeling that it might come true.

On my way to the set later that morning, I was tempted to turn up the road to Jeffrey Allman's house. But I forced myself to keep driving. After all, what could have changed there overnight? Besides, I had a sneaking suspicion that I was just looking for an excuse to put off going to the movie set. And I wasn't going to give in to a little fear.

Today was going to be my busiest day on *Stealing Thunder*. I was involved in every single scene on the schedule. By the time I arrived, there was a constant rushing sound in my ears, and my heart was beating fast.

"This is ridiculous," I said out loud as I parked the car. "I've been in plenty of dangerous situations before, and I was never afraid. There's *no* reason to be afraid now. It's just *acting*."

But as I made my way to the makeup trailer, I still felt jittery. I had no idea where the fear was coming from. It just wasn't like me to have stage fright, or any fright. Of course, this meant that whenever I tried to mention my feelings to anyone, they didn't seem to believe I was truly afraid—it was too out of character. No one would think it was possible. But here I was!

"Here's Esther!" Degas sang out as I entered the makeup trailer. He sat me down and got to work on my hair.

Pam came over and began making me up. "This

afternoon's scenes are going to be fun for me," she said.

"Why is that?" I asked.

"Because we get to age you," she explained. "It's more fun to do that than just putting on regular makeup."

This afternoon we were shooting a bunch of scenes of Esther writing in her diary. Luther and Althea, the screenwriter, had convinced Morris that it was absolutely vital to include Esther's diary in the movie. Althea had written it so that the camera would film Esther writing at different points in the story, and there would be a voiceover of what she was writing. Today we would shoot me just sitting and scribbling in the diary. Later, after all the filming was done, I would go into a sound studio and record the voiceover. Basically I would just read the script of Esther's diary entries. Then, when the editors put the movie together, my voice would be dubbed in to the scenes of me writing in the diary. It would seem as if Esther's thoughts were being said aloud as she wrote.

"Esther doesn't age too much during this movie, though, does she?" I asked Pam.

"Well, your first diary scene will take place at the beginning of the film," Pam said. "So we'll make you look younger—like a girl of fourteen or fifteen. That way, the audience will realize that Esther has kept a diary for a long time."

"You can do that?" I asked, surprised. "Make me look younger?"

"You'd be surprised what a little makeup can do," Degas said. "To make you look young, we'll make your lips look plumper and put more of a rosy glow in your cheeks. And we'll leave your hair down so you don't look as matronly as you do when Esther grows up."

I wrinkled my nose. No one had ever described me as looking *matronly* before.

"Then, in the later diary scenes, Esther grows a bit older, so we'll use the makeup to make your face look thinner," Pam went on. "People are more gaunt when they're older."

"And we'll change your hair a little for every different scene," Degas said. "And you'll wear different costumes."

"We all know it's just one day of your life sitting here and filming," Pam put in. "But when you look different in each shot, the audience will believe that all these diary-writing scenes took place days or even years apart."

"It's the magic of moviemaking!" Degas added, his eyes sparkling.

I forced a smile. Everyone else on the set was here because they loved what they were doing. They had a great time creating a whole make-believe world that people would watch and enjoy in the finished film. But I just felt sick to my stomach. Why couldn't I get into the fun of it?

After makeup and wardrobe, I went back to the trailer I shared with the Alvarez brothers and Harold Safer. Ben and Luke were already there. When I saw them, I had a quick memory of my bad dream. But their friendly smiles immediately put me at ease.

"Ready for our first scene?" Ben asked. In the morning we were shooting a scene between Esther and her brothers. I was glad that the Alvarez boys would be there to ease me into the day. I was dreading the afternoon diary scenes, when I would need to be all alone in front of the camera.

"I'm not sure," I admitted. "I don't feel ready for any of this."

"Do you want to run lines?" Luke asked helpfully.

I shook my head. "I know the lines," I told him. "That's not the problem."

"Then what is?" he asked.

"I'm nervous," I said. "I don't know how you guys do it. I always thought acting would be easy, but it's not. Every time I think about the camera, I feel self-conscious."

"Just pretend you're a little kid playing a game," Ben suggested. "All you have to do is make believe you're Esther."

I bit my lip. "It's hard to do that when there's a big camera pointed at me and twenty people standing around watching," I said. "Ever since I started working on *Stealing Thunder,* I've learned a lot about how expensive it is to make a movie. I keep thinking that if I mess up, it will cost everyone time and money."

Luke gave me a sympathetic smile. "There is a lot of pressure," he agreed. "But you have to try to forget about that when you're acting. As soon as Morris calls for action, you have to forget everything except what Esther is thinking."

"I'll try," I said. And I would. But I had a feeling it wouldn't be easy.

The morning's scene went off better than I expected, though. We were at the Rackhams' cabin on the soundstage. Mary Lupiani had dressed the set so that it looked like a cheerful family home, with a teapot on the stove and Esther's half-finished knitting on the couch. The lighting director had set up giant lamps outside the fake windows of the cabin so that it appeared as though sunlight was streaming through the glass. Luther Eldridge was there, explaining to Mary just how to position the tea service that I would use in the scene.

Looking around at the cheery "house"—and knowing that it was all historically accurate, thanks to Luther—made me feel better. Maybe I *would* be able to pretend I was Esther. As long as I blocked out the director, the cinematographer, the camera operators, and the rest of the crew, I could make believe I was a real frontier girl in a real nineteenth-century frontier cabin.

Having Luke and Ben there helped. They'd already filmed a bunch of scenes in this cabin—all the scenes of the Rackham boys planning their heist. So they were very comfortable on the set. They treated the place as if it really was their home. And as soon as they stepped into the cabin, they began acting like their characters, John and Ross Rackham. Their whole personalities changed. Instead of the sweet, fun-loving Alvarez brothers, they became the cocky, dangerous Rackham Gang.

The scene we were going to film was one in which Esther has finally discovered that her brothers are planning to do something illegal. She doesn't know exactly what their scheme is, and she doesn't know that it involves the Mahoney Anvil office. But she knows they're up to no good. In the scene Esther begs her brothers not to commit a crime. She's supposed to be terrified by their plans, and pleads passionately against them doing anything illegal.

I figured it would be easy enough to act like that. If someone I loved was planning to commit a crime, I'd be passionately against it too. I thought back over some of the mysteries I had solved. One thing I'd discovered was that not everyone felt the way I did about crime—or about family. I'd seen cases in which sisters and brothers had plotted against each other. It made me wonder how much the real Esther had known about her brothers' crime. Her diary showed that she knew *something*. But those missing diary pages still nagged at my mind. Luther had told me that people assumed Esther tore the pages out herself, to protect her brothers. But I couldn't help wondering if maybe the Rackham boys had taken their sister's diary and ripped out the pages that might incriminate them. They were true criminals—they would probably rather protect themselves than respect their sister's property.

I shook my head, trying to clear my thoughts of the old mystery. I didn't have time to think about solving it right now. I had to solve the mystery of how to conquer my own fear!

Morris gave us about ten minutes to rehearse the scene. I found that I wasn't so nervous when it was just practice. It was easy to pretend I was Esther Rackham, that this was my cabin, and that these were my brothers. But then Morris called for take one, and my heart began to pound again.

"Action!" Morris called.

Ben immediately began to pace around the cabin.

Luke just stood still and glared at me. I gazed back at him, frozen. I couldn't remember what to do. All I could think about was the camera trained on me, and all the people watching.

Luke raised his eyebrows, waiting for me to say my line. I had remembered the line perfectly in rehearsal, but now my mind was a complete blank.

"Cut!" Morris called. "Nancy, what's wrong?"

"Sorry," I said, embarrassed. "I . . . I guess I forgot the line."

"The line is, 'I know what you're up to, and I want it stopped,'" called Jenny Kane, the script coordinator. She was always on set with the latest copy of the script to make sure the actors got the lines right.

I nodded. "Okay. Thanks, Jenny."

"Good. Take two," Morris called. Ben went back to his first mark—the exact place he's supposed to be standing when the scene starts. The camera pulled back to its starting position, and everyone got ready for the next take.

Meanwhile, I could barely breathe. What if I forgot the line again? It would be just like my dream from this morning. Everyone would make fun of me!

"Hey, Nance," Luke whispered. "Just ignore the camera and all that."

"How?" I whispered back.

"Keep looking at me," he said. "And keep thinking

71

about how much you don't want me to commit a crime."

"I'll try," I said.

Morris called "Action!" one more time. I took a deep breath and stared at Luke. Ben was pacing up and down behind the couch, annoyed, but Luke just glared at me with a challenging look. His expression seemed to say that he was planning his heist and there was nothing I could do to stop him. I felt a surge of anger toward him for wanting to do something so stupid, and mixed in with the anger was fear for his welfare if he got caught.

"I know what you're up to, and I want it stopped," I said angrily. I turned to Ben, who was still pacing. "You two boys are going to get in over your heads!"

"Told you we shouldn't have let her know about it," Ben, as Ross Rackham, growled.

"She don't know a thing," Luke, as John Rackham, replied. "What are you fretting about, Esther?"

"You're planning a crime," I cried. I felt indignant— did he really think I couldn't tell when my own brothers were plotting something? "I don't know what it is, but I know it's against the law."

Luke rolled his eyes. "You're imagining things, Sissy," he said soothingly. "Ross and I would never go against the law."

I dropped my knitting needles onto my lap in

frustration. "Don't treat me like a child," I snapped. "I want you to promise me that I have nothing to worry about."

Ben and Luke exchanged a charged glance. "You have nothing to worry about," Ben mumbled guiltily. Then he turned and ran out of the cabin.

"And . . . cut!" Morris called. "That was terrific!"

I blinked, surprised to hear Morris's voice. For a few minutes there I had forgotten I was on a movie set at all! I had been completely focused on watching Luke and Ben, and on feeling what I thought Esther would be feeling. I had been able to ignore the cameras and all the people.

"See, Nance?" Luke said. "If you pay attention to the other actors, you forget to be nervous."

I grinned at him. "You're right," I replied. "That was actually kind of fun."

The rest of the takes for that scene went well. Every time I started to feel nervous, I simply forced myself to watch the Alvarez brothers. They were such seasoned actors that they always seemed to know what they were doing. Even if I felt self-conscious, I just paid attention to Ben and Luke. I didn't even try to act like Esther—I just tried to react to whatever "Ross" and "John" said and did.

By lunchtime I was exhausted. Bess joined me at the table in the mess hall.

"The whole set is buzzing about you," she said. "How you're a total pro."

I shook my head. "I'm not a pro," I told her. "I was terrified the whole time. The only reason I even got through it was because the Alvarez boys helped me."

Bess took a bite of her sandwich. "I doubt that," she said. "Some of the lighting crew came over to help us with the new Mahoney house set. They said watching you was just like watching Esther Rackham herself!" She leaned in closer. "Even Luther thinks your character is totally authentic."

"Well, I was lucky in the scene we filmed this morning," I said. "I could easily imagine what Esther was thinking. She didn't want her brothers to commit a crime. She tried to talk them out of it."

Bess's blue eyes narrowed. "Wait a minute," she said. "I thought Esther didn't know what her brothers planned to do. That's what we learned in school, isn't it?"

I nodded. "Yeah. But Luther says that her diary hints at her knowing *something*. She tore out the pages about the actual heist and what happened to her brothers afterward."

"Right," Bess said. "So why does Luther think she knew what they were planning beforehand?"

"When he read over the diary again for this production, he found a passage that he hadn't paid much attention to before," I explained. "Two days before the heist, Esther wrote that she had a fight with her brothers. All she said was that she wanted them to 're-consider.' They wouldn't, and all three of them had a fight. Then the next day's entry is torn out."

Bess nudged my arm. "Sounds mysterious," she said with a grin.

"I guess," I said. "But I'm almost too busy trying to calm my nerves to get interested in a hundred-year-old mystery!"

Bess just laughed. "Yeah, right! Well, I bet your nerves will calm down as soon as you step in front of the camera again," she told me. "You're a natural!"

I sighed. My friends just didn't seem to understand how much this stage fright was bothering me. But I really wanted to talk to them about it.

In the afternoon I returned to the makeup trailer, where Pam and Degas made me into a younger version of Esther. Then we all went over to the Rack-hams' cabin set. I could see that Mary had done some work there to make the place look slightly different than it had before. The fabric on the couch was newer and cleaner, and there weren't as many props cluttering the set.

"I'm going to re-dress the set after every scene,"

Mary explained to me. "We're just going to craft little differences, so that audiences will think it's a different day in each scene."

"And you'll be sitting in different places in the cabin for each scene," Morris chimed in. "One time you'll sit at the table to write in the diary. Another time you'll be on the couch, or in the rocking chair."

"It's hard to believe that it will look as if each scene is a different time," I said. "When I know all along that they were shot within an hour of one another."

"Okay, we're ready," Mary said. "The cabin set should look newer, as if Esther and her brothers hadn't been living there for long. There isn't as much furniture and there aren't as many decorations on the walls."

I nodded. "It definitely looks newer."

"And *you* look younger," Pam said with a proud smile. She powdered my face one last time, and then I took my place at the wooden table.

My pulse pounded in my veins as I waited for the shoot to start. I felt out of place. What was I doing, acting in a movie? I wasn't an actor—I was a detective! Solving mysteries, I could do. Helping people I could do too. But acting well? Or calming my own jitters? Not at all!

Mary's assistant handed me a leatherbound book.

Inside were blank pages made of old-fashioned pressed paper. It was one of the three duplicates of Esther's diary that the props department had made.

"Here we go, Nancy," Morris said. "You're going to write in the front section of the book. Remember, you're only fourteen years old now. You're new in the area, and your brothers are still trying to make a go at being farmers."

I nodded. It seemed strange that he wanted me to think of all that stuff when the only thing I had to do was write in the diary.

"Action," Morris said.

I opened the little book, took up the heavy fountain pen, and paused. What was I supposed to write? Suddenly I panicked. Had Morris wanted me to memorize Esther's actual diary entries? Was the camera going to show what I was writing? I had no idea what kinds of things Esther had written when she was younger. The only thing they'd taught us in school about her diary was that those incriminating pages were ripped out.

"Cut," Morris said. "Nancy? Why aren't you writing?"

"Um, I'm not sure what to write," I admitted. "Did you want me to memorize the actual diary?"

He chuckled. "Good heavens, no. I wouldn't expect anyone to do that! Just write whatever you want to."

"The camera won't see it?"

Morris shook his head. "We're not going to do close-ups yet. Later we may shoot a few takes of the entries from the real diary. I haven't decided yet."

"Okay. Sorry." I leaned back over the book as a production assistant read off the information about the scene and the take.

"Action," Morris called.

I touched the fountain pen to the page, and the black ink sank right into the paper, making a big blot. I tried to pretend I hadn't noticed. I began moving the pen, but I still didn't know what to write. In desperation I wrote down my address. Then I wrote Bess's, and then George's. The whole time all I could think about was the camera. There were at least fifteen people on the soundstage, and they were all staring right at me. The camera was watching me and only me.

I wrote down Jeffrey Allman's address. I hadn't even realized I was thinking about him, but I guess the mysterious fire at his house was still in the back of my mind. Maybe I could make a list of possible motives for someone setting the fire. But I felt kind of silly writing something like that in Esther's diary.

It was really quiet. The silence made me even more nervous for some reason. All I could hear was the sound of the pen scratching as I wrote. My breath began to come faster. I missed having the Alvarez brothers here to distract me. I noticed that my hand was shaking, and the fountain pen made another big blot.

"And . . . cut," Morris said.

I put down the pen and turned nervously to the director. "That was good, Nancy," he said unconvincingly. "But in this next take I want you to remember what we talked about. You're only fourteen, and you have no worries yet about your brothers."

"Okay," I said. But I still didn't understand why any of that mattered. We did another take. I could tell right away that this one was worse than the last one. With the camera rolling, I became completely self-conscious. I knew that my hands were moving in a weird, stilted way. I wondered if I was sitting up straight or if I would look slumped over on camera. I concentrated on straightening my spine.

Morris called cut again. He got out of his chair and came over to sit with me at the table. I winced, expecting him to yell at me for being such a bad actress.

"You need to relax, Nancy," he said gently. "You're very stiff. What's the matter?"

"I feel silly just sitting here and writing," I admitted.

Morris smiled. "Maybe that's the problem. You should be doing more than just sitting and writing."

Shoot. I was supposed to be doing something else?

Had I forgotten some of his directions? My cheeks grew hot with embarrassment. "What else should I be doing?" I asked.

"Thinking," he said. "You don't suppose that Esther Rackham felt silly sitting at her table and putting her thoughts down in her diary, do you?"

"Of course not," I said.

"So why should you feel silly?"

I thought about that. "Well, nobody was watching Esther," I pointed out. "She didn't have a camera pointed at her."

"But if you want to act like Esther, you have to think like Esther," Morris told me. "*You* might know you're being filmed, but Esther doesn't. She's just writing in her diary."

"I guess," I said. "But I'm not Esther. How am I supposed to forget the camera?"

"By thinking," he said again. "Right now, you're thinking your own thoughts—about how you feel silly, about what you should write, about what position you're sitting in. Am I right?"

I nodded. "I'm self-conscious."

"Exactly," Morris said. "So instead of thinking your own thoughts, try to think Esther's thoughts. She's not aware of what position she's sitting in. She's not wondering what words to write. She's just thinking her thoughts and putting them down on paper."

"That's why you're telling me to remember how old she is and what her current family situation is?" I asked. "So that I'll be able to figure out what she'd be thinking?"

"It will give you a starting point," he said.

I was beginning to understand what he meant. That morning I had concentrated on the other actors. By paying attention to them, I forgot to pay attention to myself and my own thoughts. Now Morris was saying that I should pay attention to Esther's thoughts the same way I'd done with the Alvarez brothers.

"I'll do my best," I promised Morris.

When we did the next take, I tried to ignore the camera. Instead I thought about fourteen-year-old Esther. She was a pioneer girl whose parents had both died when she was a toddler. As far as I could remember, she had been raised by her two older brothers. *It's odd that she didn't learn bad behavior from them,* I thought suddenly. The Rackham boys were notorious criminals, but Esther had been a good girl who saved the life of the man her brothers had tried to kill. Where had she learned her morals? Clearly not from her wild brothers.

"Cut!" Morris's voice broke into my thoughts. I jumped, startled. A glance at the diary showed me that I'd been writing down what I was thinking about

Esther. Somehow I had managed to forget my nervousness for a moment. I'd even forgotten the camera.

"Much better," Morris said happily. "Let's do it again."

My heart sank. Forgetting the camera for one take had been hard enough. How could I do it for another take? Not to mention for all the other scenes I still had to film this afternoon. I had a feeling I was in for a very long day.

Almost nine hours later, I stumbled out of my trailer, exhausted. All afternoon we had filmed Esther writing in her diary. Between every scene, I'd had to wait while Pam and Degas changed my hair and makeup to make me look a little bit older each time. Mary had to change the set, too, to make it look a little more shabby and lived-in as I grew "older." Plus, the lighting crew had to change the position of their lamps, and Morris had to decide where he wanted me sitting in each scene. But those things were all easy compared to the acting I had to do.

Sitting still and writing didn't get any more comfortable, no matter how many times I had to do it. There was something so intimate about writing in a diary—it was almost impossible to do it naturally with a camera watching. I used Morris's trick as much as I could. I thought about how Esther would feel at the age of fourteen, at the age of sixteen, after she'd gotten a job as a bank teller, while she was sick with influenza, and finally when she realized that her brothers were planning a crime. In each different scene, I thought about what was going on in Esther's life at the time. Sometimes it worked, and sometimes it didn't. All I knew for sure was that it had taken a long, long time to film.

By the time I had changed back into my own clothes and gotten my stuff from the trailer, it was almost eleven o'clock at night. There was a note on the mirror in my trailer that said there were changes to the script for tomorrow. That meant I had to go and pick up the revised script pages tonight so that I could learn the new lines in time for the next day's shoot. Yawning, I headed over to the main office. The office was in a temporary building near the parking area.

I was surprised to find George still there. She was sitting at one of the desks in the back with an intricate array of computer cables in front of her.

"Hi," I greeted her. "I'm glad you're still here. I'm supposed to pick up pages for tomorrow's scenes, but the script coordinator is gone."

"Hang on a sec," George said, not looking at me. Her fingers were flying over the keyboard on the desk. I glanced around at the mess of wires and motherboards.

I yawned. I felt exhausted and worn out by the

long, difficult day. It was hard to believe that I had to come back tomorrow to shoot even more scenes. After the mess I had made of the diary scenes, I was surprised Morris hadn't fired me on the spot.

"George, can you just print out the new pages for me?" I asked. "I had a really hard—"

"This is Jeffrey Allman's computer," George interrupted me. "I've managed to recover a few files."

"What do you mean?" I asked. "Where's his computer?"

George indicated a pile of boards and chips that looked like an electronic skeleton. "That's his hard drive," she said. "I took it out of the laptop casing, because the casing was so damaged by the fire."

"Uh-huh," I said, yawning again. I really needed to get home and go to sleep. I'd have to wake up very early to learn the new lines for tomorrow. Just thinking about it made me feel nervous all over again.

"I hooked up his hard drive to the computer here, and I think I'm making real progress," George began. The sparkle in her eyes told me that she was about to launch into a long and detailed account of how she had managed to recover the damaged files. And suddenly I knew that I couldn't take it. I was so overwhelmed by my feelings of stage fright and failure and exhaustion that I couldn't stand still and listen to George talking about computers.

"I need the revised pages," I said.

"Nance, you don't understand—"

"No, you don't understand," I snapped. "I'm tired and I'm having a really hard time on this movie, but you and Bess don't seem to get it. Every time I say I'm nervous, you act like it's a joke. But it's not. I don't care about your computers any more than you care about my stage fright. Now can you just print out the pages so I can go home?"

George stared at me, her brown eyes wide and astonished. I felt a stab of guilt. I'd never spoken to her like that before. But I was too tired to do anything about it now.

Silently George turned to the computer and pulled up the script. She hit Print, and the pages shot quickly from the printer near the door. George didn't even turn back to look at me again. I took the pages from the printer and left without saying good-bye.

7

The Mountain Lion Attack

I woke up late the next morning, as usual. The first thing I thought about was how I had snapped at George. I glanced at the clock. It was almost eight thirty. George is an early bird. She was probably at the set already. I didn't want to bother her at work, so I would have to call her later.

Thinking about George reminded me of the fire at Jeffrey Allman's house. George had mentioned that she was making progress in salvaging his hard drive. I wished again that I hadn't cut her off—she'd probably been trying to tell me something important about the mystery of who set the fire. Would Mr. Allman's laptop help us find the answer? It was possible that his old computer files from Rackham Industries would contain information leading to a suspect.

I wished I could have focused on a nice, juicy mystery like that one. It would have been much easier than trying to figure out why I was so nervous all the time on the set!

I sighed and picked up the revised script pages I'd gotten last night. I only had one scene today, in the late afternoon. But the whole thing had changed a lot since the last time I saw it. Luther and Althea seemed to keep making my part bigger every time they did a rewrite. The original scene had contained only two lines of dialogue for Esther. The revised scene had two whole pages of new dialogue for me to memorize!

There was a knock on my door, and Hannah stuck her head in.

"Morning, Hannah," I said.

She stepped inside and frowned at me, her hands on her hips.

"Uh-oh," I said. "What did I do wrong?"

"You ate the dinner I left you last night," Hannah said.

I nodded. She had left a whole plate of her meatloaf and vegetables wrapped up in the fridge. I'd been so hungry by the time I got home that I stuck it in the microwave and gobbled the entire thing. "It was delicious," I told her. "Thanks."

"You left your dirty plate sitting out on the table,"

Hannah said. "With the dirty tin foil lying next to it, and the dirty utensils on the table too."

I grimaced. How could I have forgotten to clean up after myself? Hannah hates anything dirty on the clean table. "Yikes!" I cried. "I'm sorry, Hannah. I got home so late, and it was such a bad day . . ."

Immediately Hannah's frown disappeared. She studied my face for a moment, then took a seat on the foot of the bed.

"Why was it a bad day?" she asked.

"I kind of messed up a lot during filming," I admitted.

"Did you forget your lines?"

"No." I shrugged helplessly. "I didn't even have any lines. I was just sitting there writing in a diary."

"So how did you mess up?" Hannah asked. "You never 'mess up' anything!"

"Oh, come on, Hannah. I got nervous, so I didn't look natural," I told her. "The director helped me out a lot. In fact, if he hadn't taught me a trick about how to do it, I wouldn't have gotten through a single take."

"But you still think you did a bad job?" Hannah asked. "Even after he taught you his trick?"

I nodded. "I could tell he was frustrated with me by the end of the day. They were just short scenes with no dialogue. It shouldn't have taken so long to shoot them all. But I had to keep doing a lot of takes."

"Why?"

"I got self-conscious in front of the camera," I said quietly. "In fact, I *always* get self-conscious these days."

Hannah's brow wrinkled in concern. "That doesn't sound like you," she said. "You're the most confident girl I know."

"Not when it comes to acting," I murmured.

"What do your friends say?" Hannah asked.

"Every time I try to tell anyone that I'm nervous, they say it's normal," I told her. "But I don't think it *is* normal. This is more than just jitters. I'm really afraid I'm going to make a fool of myself."

"But Bess and George said that everyone on set considers you a natural," Hannah protested.

I shrugged. "I doubt Morris thinks I'm a natural after yesterday. Mostly I've just managed to muddle through."

Hannah looked skeptical. "I have a feeling that you're doing a much better job than you think you are," she said.

"It's just such a big responsibility," I told her. "The film and the cameras are expensive, and the sets are expensive, and the salaries for all the crew members are expensive. Plus, after the rough beginning this movie had, with Herman Houseman's sabotage, everyone is working their hardest to make sure the final film is terrific."

"And you think that if you do a bad job, you'll let them all down," Hannah said. "Now I understand."

"Understand what?" I asked.

"Why you're so afraid." Hannah reached for my hand and gave it a squeeze. "You're not nervous about your acting talent. You're afraid of disappointing people—the director and the other actors and the crew."

I frowned. Could that really be the reason?

"Nancy, being afraid just isn't part of your personality," Hannah said. "But wanting to do a good job—that's your personality. Whenever there's a wrong, you want to right it. That's why you got George and Bess and Mrs. Fayne and Harold Safer involved in *Stealing Thunder*. Because the movie would have fallen apart without them, so you stepped in and found people to do the jobs that needed to be done."

I had to smile. That was true. Morris had called me his local headhunter because whenever he had a crisis, I found someone to solve it.

"But you're afraid that if you do a poor acting job, *you'll* be the one creating a problem for the film," Hannah said. "You don't want to let them down. It's a perfectly natural fear."

I chewed on my lip while I thought about that. "But how do I get over it?" I asked.

"Well, first of all, you can believe people when they say you're doing a good job," Hannah teased.

"I always think they're just being nice," I said. "But I'll try to believe them."

"And second," Hannah went on, "I have a little trick of my own that you can try."

"Really? What is it?"

"Did I ever tell you about my cousin Ethel?" Hannah asked.

I shook my head. "Are you really related to someone named Ethel?" I couldn't help but grin.

"You bet," Hannah said. "Cousin Ethel was the kind of girl who always wanted to be a star. She was outgoing and funny and charismatic, just like you."

I blushed. "You're biased, Hannah," I pointed out.

Hannah kept on talking. "So when she got to be a senior in high school, everyone assumed that Ethel would be the star of the school play. And she got the part. At first she was excited and happy. She thought it would be a snap."

"And then what happened?" I asked.

"Then rehearsals started," Hannah said. "And Ethel discovered that she hated being on stage with everyone watching her. She got nervous and flubbed her lines. She had such stage fright that she hated the rehearsals and she absolutely dreaded the actual performance."

"Sounds like me," I said. "So what did Ethel do?"

"She went and talked to a wise old woman," Hannah told me. "Our grandmother, Edna."

"What did Edna say?"

"She told Ethel that there was no point in being afraid of the audience. But Ethel still couldn't shake her stage fright. So Grandma Edna suggested that every time Ethel glanced out at the audience, she picture the people sitting there in their underwear. It's hard to be afraid of someone in their underwear."

I groaned. "That's the oldest trick in the book."

Hannah gave me a stern look. "Why do you think it's been around for so long? Because it works. Don't question Grandma Edna's wisdom."

"But that won't work for me," I said. "There's no audience."

"What about all those camera operators and production assistants?" Hannah asked. "Why don't you try picturing them in their underwear?"

I had a brief mental image of Mary Lupiani and Pam and Degas sitting around in their underwear. And, worse, Morris Dunnowitz in a pair of polka-dotted boxers and a T-shirt. Before I knew it, I was giggling uncontrollably.

"You see?" Hannah said. "Grandma Edna knew what she was talking about."

The phone rang, interrupting my laughter. Hannah gave me a smile and left the room as I grabbed for the receiver.

"Hello?"

"Nance? It's George."

Right away the laughter died on my lips. "George!" I cried. "I'm so sorry for snapping at you last night. I don't blame you for being mad at me."

"Don't be silly," George said in her typical blunt way. "Obviously you've been struggling with these jitters of yours, and Bess and I weren't helpful. No wonder you felt peeved."

"That's no excuse," I said. "I still owe you an apology."

"Apology accepted," George replied. "Now can I tell you what I was trying to tell you last night?"

"Of course," I cried. "What?"

"I hooked up Jeffrey Allman's hard drive to one of the computers here at the set. The drive had some damage, but not much. I was able to recover most of his files."

"He should be happy to hear that," I said.

"I hope so," George agreed. "But that's not the best part."

"What is?"

"I may have found a file that could help your dad. Didn't he say there was funny business with the books at Rackham Industries?"

"Yeah," I replied. "Dad is helping the new CFO look into the discrepancies."

"Well, I found a large file on Mr. Allman's hard drive. It's a spreadsheet, an accounting file. It's still corrupted, but I'm going to try to clean it up. Maybe it can help your father figure out what happened."

"Leave it to you to rescue damaged files from a burned-out computer," I said admiringly.

"I don't know if I've rescued it yet," George replied. "But I'm doing my best. And now I have a message for you from Morris."

My heart leaped into my throat. Was Morris going to fire me after all?

"He's standing right here," George went on. "And he says you're late. Get over to the set, lazy bones!"

I jumped out of bed. "On my way!" I cried.

I threw on my clothes, grabbed the revised script, and rushed downstairs. "'Bye, Hannah!" I called on my way out. "Thanks for cheering me up!"

"Remember," Hannah called back. "Underwear!"

I chuckled as I got into the car and pulled out. I drove as quickly as I could to the set. My scene wouldn't be filmed until late this afternoon, but I still needed to get there. Today and tomorrow we would be shooting all the scenes that took place in the cave outside town, where Esther found Ethan Mahoney after he was attacked by the mountain lion. The cave was a historical site, protected from developers because it was an important part of River Heights history. With the help of Luther Eldridge, we had gotten the city's permission to film there for two days.

The good news was that *Stealing Thunder* would be shot in a historically accurate location. The bad news was that the tight schedule meant we really had to rush. And because the cave was so remote, there was no parking. Everyone involved in filming was expected to travel together to the site. We were not allowed to drive our own cars because the city didn't want us parking all over the grasslands surrounding the cave. So I had to get to the production lot before the bus left for the cave location.

I was so late that I hadn't had time to practice my lines for the scene later in the day. I said them aloud as I drove. To my surprise I remembered every single new line. Not only that, but I didn't feel even the tiniest bit nervous. Maybe Hannah had cured me!

When I got to the set, almost everyone was already on the bus. I climbed quickly on board and slipped into a seat next to Bess. Harold Safer sat across from us. He was already in makeup and costume, and he looked just like Ethan Mahoney.

"Where's Morris?" I asked Bess.

"He went ahead with the camera and lighting crews," Bess replied. "They wanted to get a head start on setting up. Everything will be such a rush today."

I nodded.

"Nancy, George told me that you've been feeling really nervous," Bess said. "I'm sorry I didn't notice that you were having trouble."

I gave her a smile. "I think I'm doing okay now," I told her. "But I hope I didn't ruin the movie with my nervous acting yesterday."

"Don't worry, Nancy," Harold said from across the row. "If you were nervous yesterday, I'm just as nervous today."

"Why are you nervous?" I asked.

"Well, there's a mountain lion," Harold replied. "An actual mountain lion."

I glanced around. "The lion's not on the bus, is it?"

Bess laughed. "No. The city gave permission for three vehicles to pull up to the location: this bus, the truck with the cameras and lights, and Jake's trailer with the lions."

"You won't really be near the mountain lion, Harold," I said. "The stunt man will do all the shots with the actual lion."

"If it makes you feel better, I bet Nancy could give you tips on how to survive a mountain lion attack,"

Bess said, shooting me a grin. "She's had some practice."

It was true. One of the two big cats that had been hired for *Stealing Thunder* had jumped at me during the early days of shooting. Herman Houseman and his accomplice, Rita Clocker, had loosened the door of the lion's cage. The giant cat had leaped out at me and knocked me down.

"I don't know," I said. "That mountain lion wasn't really trying to hurt me. He just wanted to get out of his cage, and I happened to be in the way." I turned to Harold. "They're trained animals. They know better than to attack for real." I tried to sound comforting.

I knew that Harold's stunt double was used to working with animals, and our mountain lions were well trained. All the attack scenes would be shot with the stunt man, and then Morris would shoot close-ups of Harold's face with Harold pretending he'd just been mauled. Later the close-ups would be edited together with the stunt man's scenes to make it appear that Harold was the one getting attacked all along.

Harold shuddered. "Even watching someone else get attacked scares me," he said.

We arrived at the location and everyone piled out of the bus. Julie Wilson grabbed me as I got out.

"Nancy, I've got your costume in the bus," she

said. "I don't want it to get dusty and dirty out here, so I'll call you to change into it about twenty minutes before we start your scene."

"Okay," I said. "I wonder what I'm supposed to do all morning. We won't be shooting my part until much later."

"You can come keep me company for now," Harold said. "Morris says I have to watch my stunt double do the mountain lion scene so that I know what Ethan Mahoney is going through."

"That makes sense," I told him. "Because Morris will shoot close-ups of you afterward. You have to know just what position the stunt man fell in so that you can get into the same position for the close-up."

"I guess so," Harold grumbled. "I've never had to deal with wild animals working in my cheese shop."

"So I guess the glamour of moviemaking is wearing off a little, huh?" I asked him.

"No, I love it," Harold said. "But I couldn't do it all the time. This schedule is hectic. I haven't seen a sunset in at least a week."

Harold's two loves in life are sunsets and the theater. It was ironic that his acting debut was preventing him from seeing the sunsets. "So you're not going to move to Hollywood after we finish?" I asked.

"Certainly not," he replied. "I'm staying right here in River Heights. The movies can come to me."

I hid my smile as I led the way up the winding trail to the cave. It was a large cave with a wide opening. Right now most of the cave entrance was blocked by camera equipment and lights. If I peered in between two of the cameras, I could just make out Harold's stunt double. He was dressed in identical clothes to Harold's, and he had the same fake mustache glued on to his face. His hat was pulled down low to obscure his face.

"Quiet on the set!" Morris called.

Everyone nearby stopped talking.

"Action, Ethan," Morris said.

The stunt man, who was playing Ethan Mahoney for the moment, began the scene. He approached the cave from the side and walked slowly in. Ethan was walking carefully because he expected to find the Rackham Gang inside the cave. What he *didn't* expect was a huge cat.

"Action—lion!" Morris called.

Inside the cave Jake Brigham released the trained mountain lion, a large female cougar named Liz. The big cat loped gracefully across the stone floor of the cave, then leaped through the air toward the stunt man. All I saw was a flash of the cougar's tawny fur gleaming in the lights. Then the lion's giant paws landed on the man's chest, and he dropped backward. Liz fell with him, ending up on top of the poor guy.

At a sign from Jake, who stood right off-camera, the cougar bared her fangs and gave a growl that echoed off the stone walls of the cave.

"Ugh, I can't watch," Harold said, turning away.

But I was fascinated. After growling so viciously, the cat simply stood in place and waited for Jake to give it the next command.

"Cut!" called Morris.

"Liz, with me," Jake commanded, striding forward to the mountain lion. Liz paced over to meet him, and he fed her a piece of meat.

"Is it over?" Harold asked.

"Yes, it's fine," I told him. "The cat is very well behaved. She's only pretending to attack."

Harold forced himself to watch the next three takes. Finally Morris said we had enough footage of the attack. It was time for Harold's close-ups.

"Can the mountain lion be taken away first?" he asked fearfully.

"I'm going to load her back in her trailer right now," Jake answered. He led Liz away on her lead as if she was nothing but a big dog.

"Okay, let's get Harold into the cave," Morris said. Pam and Degas rushed over to powder Harold's nose and make sure his mustache was glued on tightly. Tripp Vanilli, the costume designer, and Julie did one last check of his wardrobe.

"Think you'll be able to pretend you were just attacked by a mountain lion?" Morris asked Harold.

"Definitely," Harold said. "Just watching those last few takes, I felt as if I was being mauled myself."

"Then let's get going," Morris said. He led Harold into the cave to show him where his mark was. Harold was supposed to fall to the ground in just the same place that the stunt man had done it. Then he would lie there, looking stunned and petrified. After a few takes, Pam would go in and apply some fake blood and bruises so it would seem that Ethan was beginning to bleed from the lion's scratches. Then Morris would shoot a few more takes. And after that, it would be time for my scene—the scene in which Esther finds Ethan unconscious on the floor of the cave.

I figured it was time for me to go get into my costume. I hurried back to the bus, found the garment bag labeled ESTHER, CAVE and pulled out the long dress. I quickly changed in the back of the empty bus. I stuffed my feet into the tight black button-up boots. Then I climbed out of the bus and headed off in search of Pam and Degas. They still had to do my hair and makeup. When I got back to the set, though, Morris was about to start filming with Harold. I just couldn't resist watching my friend—surely I had time for one or two takes.

I squeezed into a space behind Morris's director's chair, where I had a perfect view into the cave.

"Action!" Morris called.

Harold was being extra dramatic today. He gave a little scream, then flung himself backward. He was supposed to fall straight down to the floor, but instead, he stumbled back for a few steps, his face contorted into a mask of fear.

Then the heel of his old-fashioned shoe hit something on the ground in the cave. Now Ethan's fearful expression disappeared, and I saw a very Harold-like look of alarm on his face.

"Whoa!" he called as he tripped over the rock on the ground. Flailing his arms, he toppled over backward, hitting the rear wall of the cave.

The stone wall gave way, splitting into pieces and collapsing to the floor. And Harold kept on falling, through the wall and over a ledge that had been hidden behind it. His cry of fear faded into the darkness as he fell, and soon I couldn't hear him anymore.

There was absolute silence from everyone on the set. The only sound was the clattering of falling stone.

Harold was gone!

8

Into the Darkness

I braced myself to hear another bone-chilling scream from Harold. It didn't come.

Everyone else was still frozen in horror. I forced my feet to move—I *had* to get to Harold. I rushed into the cave and over to the deep cavern that had opened up when he fell against the wall. Skidding to a stop at the edge, I peered into the darkness. Where had this chasm come from? No one had ever mentioned such a thing in the historic cave. I couldn't see Harold, and I couldn't see the bottom. All I could see were the beginnings of steep, rocky walls . . . then nothing but black.

A burst of static finally broke the silence. I heard footsteps running toward me. It was Bess, and she already had her crew walkie-talkie out. "We need an ambulance out at the cave where we're shooting. Right away—it's an emergency!" I heard her say into the mouthpiece. There was a crackling sound, then someone answered, "I'm on it." Bess pressed the button again. "You'd better contact the fire department for a rescue team too," she added.

Good idea. I could always count on Bess in a crisis. Unfortunately it would take an ambulance at least twenty minutes to get way out here. And we needed to help Harold *now*.

I dropped to my hands and knees at the edge of the cavern and leaned down as far as I could. "Harold!" I shouted. My own voice echoed back to me. "Harold!" I yelled again. "Can you hear me?"

Silence.

My heart started to beat double-time. Harold needed help down there, and he needed it immediately. I felt a hand on my shoulder. "Nance, move back a little, okay?" Bess said. I could see tears in her eyes—she was obviously just as worried about Harold as I was. "It's making my stomach go all whoopsie seeing you that close to the edge."

"She's right. I know we're all concerned about our friend, but it's not going to help Harold for you to go tumbling in after him," Luther Eldridge agreed, hurrying up beside Bess.

I pushed myself to my feet. "I'm not tumbling

anywhere," I promised Luther, taking in his pale face and worried eyes. "But I *am* going in after him."

"Absolutely not," Morris cried. He had finally shaken off his horror and come running into the cave. I could see the rest of the crew milling about outside the entrance, trying to figure out what to do. "We already have one person down. We're not going to add you to that list!"

"You have to wait for the ambulance," Luther agreed.

"Harold wouldn't be down there if it wasn't for me," I shot back. "I'm the one who convinced him to be in the movie in the first place. And it's going to take the ambulance too long to get here."

"Nance, don't be crazy," Bess said. "I'm worried about him too. But you can't just throw yourself in there. We can't even see how deep it is, and you have no way to get down safely."

She had a point. I scanned the cave and the area outside it where the crew was set up. Rope. I needed rope. I didn't see any. But I did spot something even better: electrical cords. Tons of them. They were hooked to the cameras and to the lights and lying in coils on the ground. There was more of the heavy black cord than I could ever use!

"Bess, get me the first-aid kit," I said. I pulled up the long skirt of my costume so I wouldn't trip, then

I raced over to the nearest camera. The longest stretch of electrical cord was attached to it. In about three seconds I had the cord wrapped around my waist and tied tight. Good thing I had learned all about knots during my camping trips with my dad growing up—I knew this one would hold.

"Harry! Jim!" I cried to the two biggest grips. Grips are the people on a movie set who deal with the equipment—hauling, lifting, and moving. This would take muscles like theirs. "You two hold the other end of this." I gave the cable attached to my waist a tug. "And don't let go!"

"You can count on us," Jim answered. He grabbed the loose end of the long, long length of cord and wrapped it around his own waist. Harry stepped in front of him and took hold of the cord with both hands.

"Thanks, guys," I said. I marched back over to the lip of the cavern. The black electrical cord unspooled behind me.

"It's so dark down there," Luther said. "How are you going to see to help Harold?"

I bit my lip, thinking hard. "There's a miniflashlight in my purse," I remembered. "It's the brown leather one in my seat on the bus." Julie Wilson took off at a run toward the bus.

Bess rushed over with a large metal box. "The

first-aid kit is way too heavy for you to carry with you," she said.

I frowned. Bess was right. "Bandages are the most important thing," I told her. She handed me several Ace bandages and three rolls of gauze. I stuffed everything into the waistband of my skirt.

Julie came running up with the little flashlight from my purse. "Thanks," I said, taking it. I turned to Morris. "I'll use this for starters. You get the lights moved up here and pointed down into the cavern, okay?"

"You got it," he promised.

I glanced at Bess. She gave me a shaky smile. "Be careful."

I nodded. "Every time I give two sharp tugs, let out about five feet of cord," I called to Harry and Jim.

"Got it!" Harry called back. Jim gave me a thumbs-up.

I flicked on my little flashlight and jammed it between my teeth. As Morris winced, I made knots in both sides of my long skirt to get some of the material out of the way. Then I turned around so that my back was to the cavern. I grabbed the cord tight in both hands. Then I leaned back, letting my body hang out over the opening to the deep pit.

I stretched my left foot down and braced it against

the rock wall of the cavern. Then I started walking slowly down the side of the wall. The boots of my Esther costume gave me surprisingly good traction.

After five steps the thin beam from my flashlight was all the light I had. The darkness of the chasm pressed in around me, surrounding me in black. "Harold?" I called as well as I could with the flashlight in my mouth. There was no answer.

Fear shot through me. He could be seriously hurt. He'd been unconscious for a while now, unless this cavern was so deep that he just couldn't hear me. But chances were that he was gravely injured and needed immediate medical attention. Obviously I didn't have time to take the wall of the cavern step by step. I sucked in a deep breath, then gave the cord two sharp tugs and pushed off from the rock wall with both feet.

And I was in the air. Falling.

Suddenly Harry and Jim grabbed the cord again. I pointed my toes on the rock and used my feet to steady myself. Then I tugged the cord two times again, and took another short flight. This was another trick I'd learned while camping with Dad—how to rappel down a wall. Of course, I'd only done it outside before, in the sunlight where I could see where I was going.

Usually I love the feeling of rappelling. But now all I could think of was Harold. Was he okay down there? And exactly how far down *was* he? I had already lost track of how far down I'd gone. The darkness confused my sense of distance.

I gave Harry and Jim the signal again, and I went swooping down. A spiderweb—one that spanned a quarter of the cavern opening—came rushing up to meet me. I didn't want to go through it. And I *really* didn't want to meet the spider big enough to spin that web!

But there was nothing I could do. I felt the web's soft stickiness in my hair, then on my cheek. "Cotton candy," I told myself. "Just pretend it's nothing but cotton candy."

I tugged two more times. The sticky strands gave a lurch, then pulled themselves free of me as I sped down another length of cord. Now the web was ten feet above me.

My feet landed back on the rock wall with a thud. I paused to give myself time to pull in a couple of long breaths—and I realized something was watching me.

My flashlight illuminated two eyes peering at me from a large hole in the wall. A snake? No, the eyes were too big. Too big for a rat, too. What else would live down here? *A bat?* I wondered, picturing the wicked teeth of those creatures. Or was it something bigger?

My stomach turned over. Could it be a mountain lion? Like Liz, from the movie? The hole was big enough for a mountain lion to use as a lair. No, it was too deep. Even a mountain lion couldn't climb out of there. Right?

Whatever the thing was, I didn't want to give it time to spring out at me. I tugged twice on my cord, and once again I felt myself falling through the air. This time, though, it didn't last long. Almost immediately, the bottom of my feet smashed hard against rock. My knees buckled with the impact, and I stumbled to the ground. The flashlight fell from my mouth and bounced onto the dirt. Luckily it didn't break. The thin beam of light still shone out from where the light had landed about a yard away.

I spotted Harold instantly. He lay almost at my feet, and he was still. Much too still. With shaking fingers I untied the cord from my waist and crawled over to grab the flashlight. Then I sank down next to Harold.

Harold's eyelids fluttered when I pointed the beam of my little flashlight at his face. I felt a rush of relief. He was alive! And he was regaining consciousness.

"Nancy," he croaked as his eyes opened all the way.

"Yes, I'm here," I said. "You had quite a fall."

"I remember," he whispered.

"What hurts?" I asked him. I'd already spotted a

bump on his head the size of a golf ball. It wasn't bleeding much—just a little trickle—but it worried me.

"Everything," he admitted. "But I'm all right." He started to sit up.

I gently pushed him back onto the ground. "Stay still. An ambulance is on the way. The emergency rescue people will be here soon." I ran my hands slowly down his arms and legs, feeling for bumps or jutting bones. "Nothing broken, I don't think," I told him.

I used my flashlight to try to get a better look at his condition. The faint light didn't help me much, but I could see that one of his pant legs had been ripped open. He had the start of a nasty bruise on his bare calf, and his skin was torn and bleeding. There were little cuts and scrapes all over his arms and hands.

"So I'll live?" Harold asked. He gave a weak smile.

"Absolutely," I told him. "You'll be back selling cheese before you know it."

"I hope so," he said. "This acting thing is even more dangerous than I thought."

Suddenly the cavern was flooded with light. It was like being photographed by one thousand flash cameras all at once. It took me a moment to realize what had happened. The movie lights had been dragged into the cave and pointed down at us, just as I had asked. Morris had come through for me!

I blinked rapidly, trying to get rid of the blue and white dots filling my vision. I hadn't thought I'd ever say the cavern was too bright, but at that moment it almost was.

My eyes adjusted and I got a better look at Harold. To my relief I couldn't find any injuries I'd missed in the dim light.

"I didn't fall quite as far as I thought I did," Harold said, staring up at the mouth of the cavern high above us. "It felt as if I went about halfway to the center of the earth."

"You went far enough," I answered. "I'm surprised that you weren't hurt worse, landing on this hard ground." I looked around to see if there was something that had broken his fall.

What I saw forced the air out of my lungs in a *whoosh*.

"What?" Harold asked. "What's wrong?"

He tilted his head so he could see what I was looking at. He let out a shrill shriek of terror that made the little hairs on the back of my neck stand on end.

Two skeletons lay on the cold stone next to Harold. Their skulls were turned toward me, and their empty eye sockets stared right through me, the darkness showing through the gaping holes.

Harold screamed again, and used both hands to shove himself away from the skeletons.

"Harold, no!" I cried. "You have to stay still until the medics get here!" I gently held him by the shoulders until he calmed down.

"Sorry, Nancy. It's just that seeing those things right next to me . . ." He let his words trail off.

"I know," I answered. "I felt like I was going to jump out of my own skin!"

Harold kept himself turned away from the horrible piles of bone. But I could see curiosity in his eyes. "Are they who I think they are?" he asked without looking at the skeletons.

I took a deep breath and turned back to the skeletons. I forced myself to study them. One still wore the remnants of leather boots. The boots were almost entirely gone, but I could see the sharp silver spurs still gleaming in the light. The other skeleton lay half on top of a gun with an ivory handle. I recognized it immediately. Esther Rackham had left behind an identical gun when she died. It was in the River Heights Historical Society museum. Everyone had always assumed that it was a gift from her husband, Ethan Mahoney. But now I saw the truth—that gun hadn't belonged to Esther at all. It had belonged to one of her brothers. They must have had matching guns!

I glanced back at Harold and nodded. "The Rackham boys!" I answered. "One of them still has his gun. It matches Esther Rackham's famous ivory-handled pistol."

"No matter what else is going on, you always find a mystery to solve, Nancy," Harold said. He coughed, then winced in pain. "I guess now we know what happened to the Rackham Gang, huh? Looks like they never left town."

I nodded. "We still don't know what happened to all the money they stole, though," I said.

I gazed around the narrow chasm, shifting into sleuthing mode. Every inch of the place was now as bright as day. On the wall that I had rappelled down hung bits and pieces of old rusted chain. Clearly there had once been a chain ladder leading down to this chamber from the main cave above us. And at the bottom of the old ladder I spotted something that made my heart pound with excitement: a rotting wooden chest. At one time the chest had clearly been bound with brass, but now most of the brass joints were hanging off the ancient wood. But I knew what it was anyway. It was the chest that the Rackham boys had stolen from Ethan Mahoney's office on the riverboat. I'd seen pictures of that chest from the police reports about the Great River Heist. For a long time after the heist, there had been a poster with a picture of the chest, advertising a reward for anyone who found the stolen money.

But nobody had known that the chest was nearby the whole time—right down here in this secret cave. I stood up and walked over to look into the chest.

Empty. The money was gone!

9

Truth and Lies

Nancy, what's going on down there?" Bess shouted. She sounded as if she was a mile away, and her voice bounced around the stone shaft. "We heard screaming."

"Harold's fine!" I yelled back, my own voice echoing strangely too. "So am I. But you'll never guess who we found down here!"

"The Rackhams?" Luther asked. Even from this far away I could hear the wonder and excitement in his voice.

"Yes! Well, their skeletons, anyway," I yelled back.

"I hear the ambulance," Bess called. "We're going to meet them. We'll get someone down to you ASAP."

"Hear that?" I asked Harold. "You'll be above-ground in no time."

"Great," he answered. His eyes wandered toward the skeletons, then quickly jerked away.

I wanted to take a closer look at them—to see if there was anything else besides the spurs and the gun on their bodies. But there would be time for all that after Harold was safe aboveground.

I turned all my attention to Harold. I noticed that the cut in the center of the lump on his forehead was bleeding more heavily. I pulled out a square of gauze from the waistband of my long skirt and gently pressed it over the shallow cut.

"I want to bandage up your knee," I told him. "Can you hold the gauze in place on your head? We need to keep the pressure on it to stop the bleeding."

"Uh-huh." He slid his fingers on top of the bandage and held the gauze against his skin, which shone pale in the bright light. Poor Harold had never been much of an adventurer. This might just be the worst upheaval he'd ever had in his life.

I wrapped an Ace bandage around his slashed and bruised knee, and anchored it in place with the little metal clips attached to the bandage. "How's that feel?" I asked. "I want it to be tight, but not so much that you're in more pain."

"It's fine," he answered. "I'm just glad to have some company down here."

"I'm so sorry I got you into this," I told him. "You

would never have been in the cave if I hadn't talked you into joining the movie cast."

"Don't apologize, Nancy. Being a part of the movie is more fun than I've had in years," Harold told me. He gave my arm a pat with his free hand. "I love the cheese shop, but I needed a little adventure." He chuckled. "Well . . . maybe not quite *this* much."

I felt some pebbles hit the top of my head. Glancing up, I saw one of the emergency medical technicians begin to rappel down the wall. The EMT had a harness that looked a lot more comfy and secure than my electrical cords.

"You'll have even more company in a sec," I told Harold. I watched as the EMT swung down the wall in stages.

"Coming in for a landing," the EMT called.

I moved even closer to Harold to give her plenty of room. A moment later she hit the ground.

"You're a little too late for those two," Harold told her. He jerked his thumb at the skeletons. I felt myself relax a bit. He couldn't be too badly hurt if he was able to joke around.

"So I see," the EMT answered with a grin. The skeletons didn't seem to bother her at all. "I'm Sally LaMott. I'll be your flight attendant out of here," she told Harold. She crouched down next to him and began checking him over the same way I had. She examined his bandaged knee.

"Nice job," she told me.

Another harness was being lowered down from up above. This one had a metal cage attached to the end. I recognized it as a type of stretcher. When it reached the bottom, Sally unhooked half of the cage so that the thin metal straps that connected it to the rope hung loose. I helped her slip the straps underneath Harold's body. We pulled them through, then attached them back onto the main rope.

I put a hand on Harold's arm. "You're ready to go," I told him.

"I most certainly am," he agreed. "I can't wait to get away from those Rackham boys!"

"Lift him gently," Sally called. Someone up above began hauling him up. Sally waited until his stretcher disappeared over the top of the wall, then she strapped her own harness back on. "I'm going to go up and help them get him into the ambulance," she told me. "One of the guys from the search-and-rescue team will come down to get you out in a few minutes. Are you okay down here?"

I nodded. "I don't mind the skeletons," I assured her. "In fact, I think they're interesting."

She looked me over. "Brave girl," she said approvingly. Then she tugged her rope, and her partners up top began pulling her up the wall.

"Sally?" I called after her. "Do you think you could leave us the harnesses when you get out?" I asked. "I know Luther, our history expert, is going to want to come down here and see the remains of the Rackham boys."

"Sure," Sally answered. "We won't need the harnesses immediately, once I get your friend here in the ambulance. We have a spare set just in case we need them, anyway. Just make sure to return them."

"I will," I promised.

Luther must have hopped into the harness as soon as Sally got out of it. He came rappelling down to meet me about a minute after I saw Sally reach the top of the cavern. That didn't surprise me. I had been half expecting Luther to just jump down here to see the Rackhams!

What *did* surprise me was that Chief McGinnis from the River Heights Police Department was lowered down right after Luther.

"It's the Rackhams, all right," Luther said as he stripped off his harness. He slowly circled the skeletons, gazing at them in wonder. He turned to study the empty chest. "No money left at all," he murmured. "This changes everything!"

"It sure does," Chief McGinnis agreed from a few feet above us. He swung awkwardly down to the ground. I bit back a smile. Our police chief isn't the most agile man in town; I was astonished that he'd come down here at all. "It means that after the Rackham boys stole this money, someone else stole it from *them*!"

"No," Luther told him. "It means the person who hired them to steal it from Mahoney stole it back." He pointed up to the opening of the cavern, where Harold had recently disappeared. "*He* did it!"

"Who, Harold?" I asked.

"Harold?" Chief McGinnis repeated, baffled.

Then I realized what Luther meant. "He isn't talking about Harold," I explained to the chief. "He's talking about the character Harold plays in the movie—Ethan Mahoney."

"Right. Ethan Mahoney," Luther agreed. "It's the only thing that makes sense." He knelt down and ran his fingers lightly over the empty chest that was supposed to have held the stolen money.

"So you're saying the reason the money isn't down here with the boys is because Ethan took it back?" I asked. "I don't get it. Why would Ethan hire anybody to steal his own money?"

Chief McGinnis frowned. It looked as if he didn't get it either.

"It wasn't his own money," Luther reminded me.

"Oh, that's right!" I cried. I felt as if my brain had been flooded with the bright lights we used for filming. "The money really belonged to the railroad, didn't it?" I turned to Chief McGinnis. "Ethan Mahoney got paid in advance for a big anvil order," I explained. "But after the robbery, he supposedly didn't have enough money to make the anvils, or to repay the railroad the money they had already paid him."

"Ah," Chief McGinnis said. "So Ethan got to keep the money without ever delivering the goods. And no one could blame him, because he claimed to have been robbed by the Rackham Gang. Clever."

"I'm sure Ethan promised a share of the money to these poor fellows." Luther shook his head as he looked down at the skeletons of John and Ross Rackham. "But he double-crossed them."

"Killed them, you mean," Chief McGinnis said.

"Dead men tell no tales—isn't that the saying?" I asked. "This way, Ethan was sure that no one would ever find out the truth." Something itched at the back of my brain. "But what about the mountain lion attack? And Esther?"

"I always had a hard time believing that Ethan was attacked by a mountain lion," Luther said slowly. "It was the one part of the story that never made sense. A mountain lion would be a very long way from home around River Heights. Even back in Ethan's time."

"True," Chief McGinnis agreed. "We don't have cougars in this neck of the woods."

"But something happened to Ethan," I argued. "He had injuries that people saw, didn't he? The mountain lion story had to come from somewhere."

"Well, we know Ethan and Esther got married," Luther said. "We know that the town believed Ethan was attacked by a mountain lion, and that Esther saved him. That much is documented in the story that ran in the paper, and in diaries of other people who lived in River Heights at the time."

"All right. So let's assume that Esther was here with Ethan," I said. I felt as if an electric current was running through my veins. Nothing is more thrilling than trying to figure out a mystery. "Let's assume that much is true."

"Okay, I'm Ethan," Luther said. "I just killed your brothers so I can have all the money for myself. You show up in the cave. How would you act?"

I backed away. Then I moved toward Luther, pretending I had just arrived in the cavern to find my brothers lying on the ground with Luther/Ethan standing over them. I tried to get into Esther's skin, just the way I had when I was acting.

"You killed my brothers!" Rage and pain filled

me. I raced at Luther. "I hate you!" I pounded lightly on Luther's chest. I didn't want to hurt him. But I definitely thought Esther would be hitting Ethan right about now.

"Hold it right there," Chief McGinnis interrupted. "Maybe you're on to something. Far-fetched as it is, do you think Esther could be the mountain lion?" he asked Luther.

"You mean that *Esther* is the one who attacked Ethan?" Luther asked.

I curled my hands into claws. "I could probably get some pretty good scratches in." I glanced around the cavern and picked up a rock with a sharp edge. "Or what if I—I mean, Esther—used something like this?"

"The edge of that rock could easily slash through a man's skin," the chief said. "In fact, a woman with a weapon like that could probably kill a man."

"That's it!" Luther burst out. "Esther came at Ethan. Surprised him. She almost killed him with a rock, or some other kind of weapon."

"Maybe she used the ivory-handled gun she took from the body of one of her brothers," I suggested.

"But then how did Ethan stop her?" the police chief asked.

"A deal," Luther suggested. "We know Esther and Ethan ended up married. What if Ethan offered to marry her and split the money?"

"And that's why they never let anyone in their house," I said, thinking out loud. "Maybe their house was filled with all kinds of expensive things. And Esther got to enjoy them all her life."

"And that's how Ethan's ancestors ended up with so much money. Because Ethan never lost his money. He and Esther kept it," Luther added.

We grinned at each other. "I think we just solved a mystery here," I said. "Except I still want to know why Esther was in here in the first place. That part of the story has always bothered me, even when I thought the part about Ethan being attacked by a mountain lion was true. Why was Esther here?"

I looked over at the skeletons of the Rackham brothers. "I wish you two could talk. You could tell us everything."

"Chief, is there any problem with me taking the gun and the spurs off the skeletons?" Luther asked, kneeling down by the bones. "They really should be in a museum."

"I'd like to leave everything here for now," the chief answered. "It *is* a crime scene, after all—even if it is an old one."

Luther started to stand. "What's that?" I asked.

"What?" Luther replied.

"That white thing just under the handle of the gun," I answered. My fingers were itching to leap over there and grab it, but I waited for Luther to pick it up.

"A few pieces of paper," he told me as he pulled out some aged papers that had been sticking out of a leather pouch. Luther carefully unfolded them. The paper was so old that it was torn in some places along the folds. Luther's eyes widened. "It's part of Esther's diary—the lost pages!"

"Does she say why she was here? Does she explain?" I eagerly demanded.

"It seems our Esther was even less innocent than we thought," Luther said, his eyes quickly scanning the pages. "She married Ethan knowing he killed her brothers, and this says she knew all along that her brothers were planning the heist. And she knew they planned to hide out here after the heist!"

"I *knew* there had to be a reason she was in here," I said. "I knew it couldn't just be a coincidence."

"Esther was going to bring her brothers food and water until the cops stopped looking for the robbers. Then the three of them were going to leave town with the money," Luther continued.

"And when Ethan ruined that plan, Esther teamed up with him." I shook my head. "She was cold-blooded, wasn't she?"

Chief McGinnis nodded. "Sounds like she and Ethan deserved each other."

"Yoo-hoo!" Bess shouted into the cavern. "Are you ever coming back up?"

"You two go," the chief said. "I'll stay here and secure the crime scene."

Luther and I strapped on the harnesses and slowly made our way up the side of the cavern wall. Bess wrapped me in a tight hug when I finally reached the top.

"*Eww.* You've got gunk all over you," she said when she let me go. She pulled a tissue out of her pocket and started wiping the pieces of spiderweb off my face.

"Thanks. I forgot all about that. You're not going to believe what we found down there," I began.

But before I could say another word, George burst into the cave. Her cheeks were flushed and her eyes were shining.

"You're not going to believe what I found out!" she cried. "He was stealing from his own company!"

10

No More Movie

I know," I told George. "He was stealing from his own company and keeping the money for himself."

"Right!" George answered. "He laundered the money by buying antique furniture. Then he'd sell the furniture privately for a great price and buy cheap copies."

"Wait," I said. "Ethan Mahoney was buying antique furniture? What?"

"Who's talking about Ethan?" George asked. "Jeffrey Allman was buying the antiques!"

George and I stared at each other for a moment, confused. "You'd better start over," Bess suggested.

I forced my mind back to Jeffrey Allman and his antique furniture. Suddenly all the pieces fell into place. "You mean you found something on his laptop?" I asked. "Was it that spreadsheet file you told me about—or *tried* to tell me about?"

"Laptop? What laptop?" Chief McGinnis looked at me sharply. I couldn't let him think I let George take anything from the crime scene—he'd never understand. And he never seemed to get over feeling threatened by me. I signaled George to keep talking, hoping to avoid the topic.

"Yup, the spreadsheet." George smiled. "I found two different accounting files on the hard drive. That's how I found out about the furniture scam."

"Back up. What scam?" I asked.

"Remember that armoire from O'Reilly Brothers that you told us about?" George asked. "The only piece of furniture that was saved from the fire?"

"Of course," I answered. "I thought it was so strange that he had a cheap piece of furniture mixed in with his antiques."

"It turns out his whole house was filled with cheap stuff," George told me. "He'd already sold all the expensive antiques he bought."

I clapped my hand to my mouth. "Insurance fraud," I said. "He was going to claim that all the antiques were lost in the fire and collect a ton of money!"

"And he already *had* a ton of money from selling the antiques," Bess chimed in.

"Right—the antiques he bought with money he stole from Rackham Industries," George confirmed. "I even have a lead to the account numbers for the foreign banks where I believe Jeffrey kept the money until he laundered it."

Chief McGinnis seemed to mull over the information for a moment. "Hmm. Interesting. Sounds like I have a search warrant to get," Chief McGinnis said as he climbed out of the cavern in his harness.

"I'll get you Jeffrey Allman's hard drive," George told him. "It has all the info you'll need."

"I guess nothing changes," I said to Bess as George and the chief headed out of the cave. "Ethan Mahoney was pulling the same kind of scam all those years ago. Stealing from his own company."

"Attention, everybody!" Morris called.

"Yikes," I said. "I hope he doesn't want to get started on my scene right away. I definitely need some makeup help." I untied the knots I'd put in my skirt to keep it out of my way, and Bess and I walked over to join the group surrounding our director.

"We need to get this equipment packed up and the costumes back to the shop," Morris announced. "Then all of you have a week off. At least."

"At *least*?" I asked.

"Well, we're not going to be able to film in this cave for a while." Morris swung his arm toward the gaping cavern that now filled the back of the cave. "And it turns out that we have the heist story completely wrong. At least the end of it. That means more rewriting and reshooting."

Morris let out a sigh as he looked out at the cast and crew. "It also means more money. A *lot* more money," he admitted. "As you know, there have already been a lot of production problems on this shoot. I'm honestly not sure if we're going to have enough in the budget to continue."

"Oh, no," Bess whispered.

I felt my heart sink down to someplace near my stomach. "This is awful," I said to Bess. "Everyone has worked so hard."

And I'd been having fun. I was shocked to realize it, but I had. Sure, I was nervous every time I got in front of the camera. But I was finally starting to get the hang of the acting thing, and I wanted to keep working on it.

Now it looked like my acting career would be over before I'd even finished the movie!

After Morris's announcement we all took the bus back to the compound. One by one, cast and crew members headed off to their cars for the lonely drive home.

"Let's go get lunch before we head home," George

suggested. "I want to hear all the details about Nancy's archeological dig."

We all piled into my car and went to a local diner for sandwiches. By the time we started back to the soundstage to pick up my friends' cars, I had realized that there was one more loose end to the mystery of the Rackham Gang and Ethan Mahoney that needed to be tied up.

"I have to make a detour, okay?" I asked Bess and George on our way to the production compound.

"An ice cream kind of detour?" Bess asked hopefully.

"I wish," I answered. "I want to stop by Mrs. Mahoney's. We have to tell her what we found out about her family. And I think we should do it in person."

"Good idea," George said. "Not fun, but a good idea."

Not fun was right. I was still trying to figure out what words I should use to tell Mrs. Mahoney that her husband's ancestor was a thief and a murderer when we pulled into the long circular driveway in front of her gigantic house.

"Everybody out," I called. I needed moral support if I was going to do this. Mrs. Mahoney is one of my favorite people in River Heights, and I hated the fact that I was going to upset her.

We all climbed out of the car. I led the way up to

Mrs. Mahoney's door and rang the bell. The elderly lady gave a bright smile when she saw us standing there. I wondered how long the smile would last when she found out the reason for our visit.

"Oh, hello! What a nice surprise, Nancy, Bess, George. Please come in, come in," Mrs. Mahoney told us. "I don't bake—I'm not that kind of old lady." She patted her short gray hair. "But I did just buy some wonderful ginger snaps at the store. Perfect for dunking. Would you like some, girls?"

My stomach turned over at the thought of food. I knew I wouldn't be able to eat anything until I told Mrs. Mahoney the bad news. But Bess was already nodding.

At least the cookies and tea gave me a little more time to think of how I wanted to break the news. Unfortunately, a *little* more time wasn't enough. I still didn't know what I wanted to say when we were all seated in Mrs. Mahoney's grand dining room with the goodies laid out in front of us. I took a sip of my tea, buying even more time.

"So what can I do for you girls?" Mrs. Mahoney finally asked. "Nancy? Are you raising funds for one of your charities, dear?"

"Um . . . no," I said. I do work with a few different charities in River Heights, and I can always count on Mrs. Mahoney to help out, whether I'm collecting for the animal shelter or the children's art museum. She's willing to donate to any worthy cause.

"Nancy found out something about Ethan Mahoney," George blurted out.

"Ethan?" Mrs. Mahoney repeated. "You mean Ethan Mahoney, my husband's ancestor?"

"That's the one." I sucked in a deep breath, then started to talk. "I'm sorry to tell you this, Mrs. Mahoney, but Ethan wasn't quite the person you probably think he was. I know he's a beloved member of your family, but . . . well, it, um . . ." I had to just spit it out. "It turns out that he hired the Rackham Gang to steal the money from his safe. Then he killed them and took the money back. Esther Rackham knew about the whole thing. In fact, it's likely that she only married him because she wanted a share of the cash."

There was a brief silence. Mrs. Mahoney frowned at me, trying to understand everything I'd just said so quickly. I leaned forward, ready to comfort her. But then the woman started to laugh.

I shot a look at Bess and George. They seemed as confused as I was.

"That's priceless," Mrs. Mahoney said when she finally stopped laughing. "My late husband was so proud of his family fortune, and he only had it because he was related to a true villain!"

Bess reached out and patted Mrs. Mahoney's hand. "No one will blame you for what Ethan and Esther did."

"They'd better not," Mrs. Mahoney declared. "I'm only a Mahoney by marriage."

"And you don't mind if the whole story comes out in the movie—*if* there ends up being a movie?" George asked.

"Not at all," Mrs. Mahoney answered. "It'll make a much better picture, if you ask me."

"You're right!" Bess cried. "And, Nancy, now you'll have a really meaty part. An honest-to-goodness femme fatale."

"True," I answered, smiling. I liked the idea of playing someone wicked. "If we make the movie now."

"But I told you I don't mind a bit," Mrs. Mahoney said. "Don't stop just to respect my family—tell the truth."

"I know," I told her, smiling. "But rewriting the script and shooting new scenes might put us too far over budget."

"Really? Well, I can fix that." Mrs. Mahoney reached into her purse and pulled out a checkbook. Then she started to laugh again. "Imagine, my husband's money paying for a movie that spills the beans about how bad his ancestors really were. I love it!"

She wrote out the check and signed it with a flourish. Then she handed it to me. I felt my eyes go wide as I saw the amount.

"Thanks, Mrs. Mahoney. We'll get this over to Morris Dunnowitz right now," I told her. "And we'll make sure you get a front-row seat at the premiere!"

"I wouldn't miss it," Mrs. Mahoney said as she showed us out.

George, Bess, and I piled back into my car, and ten minutes later we were back at the movie compound. We ran straight to Morris's office.

"Look what we got for you!" I cried, waving the check as I rushed inside without knocking. "Mrs. Mahoney gave us money for the movie!"

Then I realized Morris had a visitor. "Oh!" I cried, shoving the check back into my pocket. "I'm so sorry. I'll wait outside."

"Not at all," said the man sitting across from Morris. "Your news sounds much too exciting to wait."

"Nancy, this is Peter Wyszinski," Morris said.

I recognized the name immediately. "You're the new CEO of Rackham Industries," I said as I reached out to shake Mr. Wyszinski's hand. "I'm Nancy Drew," I told him.

"Ah, Carson's daughter," Mr. Wyszinski said. "I'm pleased to meet you."

"You might want to make that *very* pleased," Morris suggested. "Nancy's a sleuth extraordinaire. I suspect she's the one who found those millions that belong to your company."

I shook my head. "No, that would be my friend George here," I said. I grabbed George's arm and pulled her forward. "George is a computer wiz. She did some digging in Jeffrey Allman's hard drive and found those overseas accounts where he stashed the cash that he stole from Rackham Industries."

"Well then, you have my unending gratitude," Mr. Wyszinski told George. "You've saved my company from going bankrupt during the first month I'm in charge of it!"

"Mine too," Morris said. "George, because of what you did, Mr. Wyszinski is investing in our movie, so we can finish it."

"Oh, that reminds me!" I cried. I pulled Mrs. Mahoney's check back out of my pocket and handed it to Morris. "Mrs. Mahoney wants you to have this—it's another donation toward making the movie."

Morris took it with a big smile. "Thanks, Nancy. I'll go see her tomorrow to thank her in person."

"And here's something just for you." Mr. Wyszinski handed George a check for one thousand dollars. One thousand! You could have heard her squeals of joy all the way down in the bottom of the river cave.

George turned to me immediately. "I'm giving

you a hundred dollars for those sneakers you paid for," she told me.

"And you'll be giving the rest to me, for safekeeping," Bess informed George. We all know how irresponsible George is with money.

"As long as you promise not to embezzle it," George teased. Everyone laughed.

"Hey, what is everybody standing around for?" I asked. "We've got a script to rewrite! And it's going to have some juicy lines for me."

It probably meant *lots* of juicy lines. But the idea didn't scare me. "I'm not going to let you down," I told Morris. "A thief and a villain—*that's* a role an actress-detective lives for. I can't wait!"